Revealing Wife in France

Zara Lynne

For M

Revealing Wife in France
by
Zara Lynne

Revealing Wife in France is the story of how a couple, on an extended trip to the south of France, pursue their erotic desires. Matt soon discovers that his yearning to show off and share his wife Anne is wantonly embraced by his once demure spouse. Matt is, however, unable to quell the jealousy in the pit of his stomach. Will their erotic adventures bring them closer together or tear them apart?

Visit Zara Lynne on Amazon: *www.amazon.com/author/zaralynne*

Revealing Wife in France © 2012 by Zara Lynne

Cover Design © 2012 Demurely Seductive Publishing

Cover Image © 2012 Nora Liskina

ISBN 13: 978-952-5825-06-0
ISBN: 952582506X

www.DemurelySeductive.com

PART ONE
Sheer Control

1-1. Stirrings

Jealous, that's what I was, jealous.

We had been in Aix en Provence, a delightful old town in the south of France, for almost a week now. I'd been seconded to a project in Marseilles for six months and I had managed to persuade Anne to come with me on what, for her, would be a six month holiday in the sun.

During our 15 years together, Anne had become accustomed to my long absences and had rarely been able (or even inclined) to tag along. She preferred to pursue her own career and stay close to family and friends while I clocked up the air miles and spent weeks and occasionally months overseeing company projects in far flung places.

This time was different. Anne was in-between jobs, adored France and French culture and was keen to brush up her French. She absolutely jumped at the chance. It was, in fact, her idea to rent a villa just outside Aix (rather than suffer in an apartment in Marseilles), just up the road from the house where Cézanne had once lived and painted many of his masterpieces.

I had trusted her judgement and she had been so right. The setting was incredible. The views over Mont Ste Victoire were stunning and the weather since our arrival the previous week had been perfect.

Something else of note were the changes I had noticed in my

wife. They were subtle, but no less stunning. The warm weather was, no doubt, a contributing factor, but we had been like honeymooners for the last week and Anne had taken to going out wearing short skirts, skimpy tops and sexy bras that accented her cleavage. I had often encouraged her to dress like this at home without effect, so this change in my darling wife was a welcome bonus and I was making the most of it.

But suddenly, here I was feeling stabbing pangs of jealousy. We were strolling through the back streets on our way to have a drink at one of the many cafés lining the Cours Mirabeau. Anne had just popped in to a small shop to look at some locally made jewelry. I could see her talking animatedly to the shop assistant, a young Tunisian or Algerian, who was attentively showing her various necklaces and persuading her to try them on. As she leaned over the counter to look more closely, I became aware of the young man's eyes ogling Anne's cleavage. From the angle he was standing, I could only imagine how much of my wife's breasts he could see under her loose-fitting top. From the side, I could see the outline of her breast. It was a mesmerizing sight to me, her husband. I could only imaging what the young man was thinking as he saw both of them in the flesh right before his eyes.

The assistant was quick to pull his eyes away from my wife's cleavage as she looked up to ask something about the necklace. She probably had no idea of the effect she was having on the young lad, or me, for that matter.

The more I watched the young man's eyes stealing lustful

helpings of Anne's soft breasts, the more I realized my pangs of jealousy and the apprehension in my stomach were only a precursor to the stirrings of my own lustful thoughts. The realization that I was enjoying the his lecherous eyeing of my wife hit me full force as I felt my erection stiffen at the thought.

Anne skipped out of the shop with her purchase round her neck. The chain was quite long and the silver charm hung provocatively above the cleft in her cleavage between her breasts. The attentive assistant had insisted on fastening it round her neck himself and to her delight had given her a huge discount. She was pleased with herself and kissed me passionately on the lips before we set off hand in hand down the street.

I wasn't sure what to think. I was unbelievably aroused by the thought of Anne being ogled, yet in the pit of my stomach, I had feelings of fear and jealousy. I had to admit though, I was looking forward to a similar situation happening again, and soon.

As we walked down the old streets, the jealousy hit me again. What if Anne had shown her breasts on purpose. Was she looking for something she couldn't get from me? I put the thought to the back of my mind and decided to just enjoy my lovely wife who was bubbling with happiness as we strolled in the sun to the café.

1-2. Plans

While we had been sitting on the café terrace watching the thousands of people milling by, I couldn't help but glance at the woman sitting next to me. I had tried to look at her with a stranger's eyes. What I saw was a woman pushing 40. A sensual, beautiful woman who oozed sex. Her mid-length blonde hair caressed her shoulders and her C-cup breasts were firm and full. Her cleavage was deliciously visible through the open buttons of her top. Her long, tanned legs were firm and well-toned after years of playing various sports. And finally, her blue eyes seemed to be continually smiling, even when her soft lips hinted at a frown.

It's true, I was madly in love with her and endlessly craved her body.

But now, looking through a "stranger's" eyes, I became aware that it wasn't only my love for her that made me desire her. I could see how other men might covet her too. I was rising to the thought of how sensual it was when my darling wife showed her charms to others. Despite the jealous pangs in my gut, I kept returning in my mind to the look of lust in the shop assistant's eyes and latent fantasies about Anne and another man began to surface in my thoughts.

Thinking about all this while walking back to our villa in the hills above Aix, I was totally distracted by my thoughts. So much so, that Anne even asked me if I was feeling ok. I assured her I had never felt better and that I was actually thinking about a stunningly sexy woman and how I wanted to make love to her when we got back to the villa. She even blushed at my words, but stopped and flung her arms around my neck and gave me another passionate kiss. I could feel my desire rising and ran my fingers under her loose top and lightly caressed her nipple through her bra. She kissed me even more forcefully, then took my hand from under her shirt, but instead of scolding me (as she might have done at home) she smiled and told me to hurry up. We almost ran the last stretch of road to the villa and we were quite breathless after coming up the hill.

Once inside, Anne slammed the door behind us, turned to face me, knelt down in front of me and pulled my pants open. She roughly pulled them down and freed my raging hard-on from the confines of my boxers. Less than 60 seconds after entering the villa, her soft lips were around my cock and her tongue was sending me wild. I was desperate to cum, but desperate not to. I wanted to savor this for as long as possible.

I'm not big, but neither am I particularly small. Normally Anne just takes me into her mouth as far as the ridge, but today she was reaching at least half way down the length of my shaft. I was in ecstasy and could feel myself beginning to cum. Like the gentleman I am, I told her I was getting close, expecting her to immediately pull back and finish me off with her hand. But she didn't pull back, she actually intensified her movements. As the first spurts were about to explode into her mouth, I gave her a final warning. Just as the first stream of cum was bursting from my cock she pulled me out of her mouth and directed the warm spurts over her neck and cleavage. At the back of my head I felt a twinge of disappointment that she still hadn't let me cum in her mouth, but I was too overcome by the force of my ejaculation to let it linger.

After she had squeezed the last drops from my cock, I pulled her up and kissed her. She wriggled free, pulled off her top, wiped her neck and chest with it, then dragged me into the bedroom. I pushed her onto the bed and dived between her legs, roughly pushing her panties to one side to reveal her sopping wet pussy. I plunged my tongue in and slurped up her juices. She squirmed as I sucked and licked her labia, occasionally sticking my tongue as far into her as I could. Her breathing told me she was having mini-orgasms and her hands were frantically pulling my head up to her clit. My tongue flicked and teased the little bud for several minutes, before I took the whole of her clitoris into my mouth and clamped down hard on it. She absolutely exploded. I maintained the pressure with my lips and tongue as she bucked and squealed in orgasm. I held on even after her main orgasm had subsided and let the aftershocks cascade through her body. She spasmed and shook as the orgasm subsided. I quickly removed my mouth and clamped my hand on her pussy to maintain the pressure and cause further aftershocks.

It took several minutes for her body to calm down. As she relaxed I scuttled up next to her, put my arms around her and just cuddled her close. We were both hot and sweaty from the exertion. We lay like that in silence for several minutes just enjoying the moment.

"Wow," she said finally, "that was intense. I haven't cum so strongly for years."

I was little taken aback by her words and tried not to take them as a reproach, knowing that all she meant was that today had been even more intense than normal. But coupled with my feelings of jealousy earlier, the young shop assistant's ogling and now this, I was feeling a little vulnerable and moved off the bed and into the bathroom. I splashed some water on my face and had the obligatory post-coital pee. On my way back to the bedroom, I picked up my underwear and pants and pulled them back on.

Back in the bedroom, Anne had already pulled on her silk robe and was coming towards the kitchen. She pecked me on the cheek as she passed and offered me a cold beer from the fridge.

We both went and sat on the patio at the back.

From the patio there was a great view almost to the sea, way in the distance, or so I imagined, and it was a perfect spot for enjoying both sun and shade. Anne had already made good use of it to put on a decent tan since our arrival. The patio was almost totally private. The only spot overlooking our patio was in the adjoining villa, but only from the upstairs balcony. The one person we had seen in the villa was an elderly gentleman. We had greeted him politely as he was coming out of his villa, like you should in France. He had smiled a friendly "bonjour" and raised his hat to us before walking off in the direction of the hills above the town.

We both sipped on our beers and looked into the distant landscape, lost in our own thoughts. Without thinking, I suddenly blurted out, "I was jealous, today".

Anne looked at me, "What!" she exclaimed. "When? Why?"

I felt a bit foolish having said it out loud, but did my best to explain. "Didn't you notice the shop assistant ogling your breasts?" I said. She was incredulous. "Oh, Matt, don't be so ridiculous. He couldn't have been more than 20. Why would he be ogling me? I'm almost 40, for heaven's sake. And why would that make you jealous, anyway? I thought you liked me dressing more sexily."

"Oh, God, Anne, I do, I really do. It's difficult to explain. I was jealous, but I was even more aroused by his attentions." Anne gave me a look of incredulity. "Aroused?"

"Yes, Anne, aroused. I was fiercely proud of how beautiful and sexy you are and wanted the young man to be able to enjoy looking at your body. The thought of him getting hard as he stared at your breasts was incredibly arousing. It made me desire you even more than I normally do."

Anne hadn't taken her eyes off me while I poured out my heart to her. Without saying a word, she suddenly got up and went into the villa. I thought I must have upset her, but she soon reappeared with a bottle of Pineau. She poured two glasses of our favorite tipple, a delicious mixture of cognac and fermented grape juice from south-west France, and handed a glass to me.

"So what you're saying is that you get turned on when someone looks at me?"

"Well, if you want to put it like that, yes, I do, very much so."

She looked at me again, then smiled. "I'm very flattered that you think men are looking at me, even young men, but I think you are being deluded by your own fantasies about me."

"Oh, Anne," I said, "you are incredibly sexy. Your breasts are lovely, you have long, toned legs, your bottom is round and firm and I adore your shoulders and neck, your soft, luscious lips, the smile in your eyes…"

"Matt, just stop it. That's your opinion. You have this idealized view of me even after 15 years of marriage. I look in the mirror, I know what I see. I see the real me, wrinkles, saggy breasts, flabby tummy, the works… You don't have to say these things to get me into bed, you know. I will sleep with you."

I was feeling exasperated and took a few sips of my drink, before speaking again.

"Ok, let me prove it to you. Let me prove that other men find you very attractive."

"What, you're going to conduct a survey, are you. Go around asking everyone whether I am sexy? Don't be absurd."

"No," I said, "not a survey as such, but we will find out the truth and you will soon realize that I'm right."

"I still don't understand how this will work," Anne said, "but if it will make you happy."

"It will, it will." I said, with all sorts of images flashing through my mind.

"So what do I do? She said.

Here was my chance. How far could I push this, I wondered.

"Look, we have another 10 days or so until I start the project. Before the project starts I will prove to you that men find you attractive. Not just men my age, but young men, old men, all men."

"Ok," she said, "but how?"

"All you'll have to do, is dress as I say and do as I say for the next 10 days and I will set up scenarios that prove absolutely that men are turned on by you."

"And if they're not, what then?"

"If I can't prove it, then I will take you on a 2 week holiday anywhere in the world you want."

"Wow, you must be feeling confident. So, what you're saying is, I dress like you say and do what you say for the next 10 days and you set things up to prove how attractive I am to men. No pressure to do anything I don't want to and I can pull out at any time."

"Hmm," I said, "that would be too easy for you. I'll give you three chances to veto something you don't want to do, but otherwise you have to see it through to the end, come what may. And you know I wouldn't do anything to hurt you."

She poured herself another glass of Pineau and took a drink, before looking me in the eye and said, "I can see you're serious about this. I'm not sure exactly what you have in mind, but we're in France, in the sunshine, we have 10 days to enjoy and I'm feeling particularly reckless today, so I'll do it. When do we start?"

"Right now, of course." I said. "We're going to have an amazing 10 days. Why don't you go and have a shower and I'll pick out something for you to wear. We could go into town and try out the Moroccan restaurant we saw yesterday."

Anne finished her drink, leant over to kiss me and scuttled off into the villa. "This is going to be interesting," she said as a parting shot.

Little did either of us yet realize, how interesting it would be.

1-3. Proof

After Anne had gone for a shower, I quickly downed my drink and went back into our bedroom to decide what she should wear. Ready for her on the bed I laid out my favorite white blouse, the short skirt she'd been wearing that day, a black thong, a black semi-transparent balcony bra, black pull ups and a pair of heels. I now sat in the corner waiting for her to finish in the shower.

She came into the room in her robe and immediately saw that I had placed some clothes on the bed.

"So, we're really going to do this, are we?" she said, smiling in my direction. She came over to me and sat on my lap. She then gave me a very hot kiss on the lips.

"Just to put you in the mood," she said and went over to the bed.

"A black bra," she said, looking at me, "With this blouse? Are you sure?"

"Absolutely," I said. "Everything you need is on the bed"

"If you're sure, but in that top, the bra will be clearly visible. The blouse is quite sheer. And the bra's quite transparent too, so in certain lights my nipples could be on display"

"I certainly hope so," I quipped. "I love the way the sheer blouse shows off the contrasting bra. And you have the most delicious nipples and areolae, so hopefully you'll be in the right light and

I'll get to see them!"

"Well, if you're absolutely sure that's what you want," she giggled, "because it won't only be you that will get to see them," and dropped her robe as she started putting on the clothes I'd prepared.

I was surprised. I had been expecting more resistance.

I sat and watched her in silence. I could never resist watching her dressing or undressing. I find it intensely erotic watching clothes go on and come off. Even better is when I'm the one undressing her - that really excites me.

After she had dressed she went and put on some light make-up and did her hair. I had asked her to tie it up so that I could see her gorgeous neck.

When she appeared again, I asked her to do a quick spin and just had to complement her. The bra definitely showed through her blouse, but I couldn't see her nipples - at least in this light. Her skirt was short, but came down to at least 4 inches below the tops of her pull-ups. The whole ensemble was topped off by her favorite heels. Not very high, about 2 inches, making her about 5 feet 10, but they really made her long legs look even longer, even more toned.

She really was stunning. I would have no problem proving my case.

The evening was quite warm for April, even in the south of France, but Anne asked if she could possibly put on a jacket or a shawl, just in case.

I knew she wanted it purely as a prop to help ease her fears about the sheer blouse and black bra, so I allowed it.

I got ready in a typical manly way. I threw on a clean polo shirt, grabbed my wallet and we were ready.

As we stepped out of the front garden we bumped into our neighbor. Once again he smiled, raised his hat and gave us a cheery "bonsoir". This time, however, he didn't just walk on by, he stopped for a chat. His French was clear and moderately slow, so even I could make out what he was saying. Once he realized that Anne was the linguist of the two of us, his attention turned very much to her. He was exceedingly charming, probably about 60 years old, and even complimented Anne on how beautiful she looked. She blushed profusely, pulling her Pashmina more tightly about her, and seemed to feel the need to invite him over for drinks the following evening.

After more pleasantries and reconfirmation about drinks, we took our leave and strolled arm in arm towards the town like young lovers. Anne was particularly excited and chatted animatedly all the way to the restaurant about everything and nothing.

The restaurant was quite busy as always, but they managed to fit us onto a table for two in a quiet alcove near the back. The decor was authentic Moroccan with rugs and artifacts on the walls. Although the restaurant itself was quite large, with the clever use of pillars and alcoves, it offered privacy to a large proportion of the diners. Only the tables in the centre of the space were in full view of everyone.

Our waiter was young and very attentive. He offered to take Anne's Pashmina, but she said she'd hang on to it for the moment, but I said I thought she might be a little hot and gave her a stern look.

She took the hint and handed over her safety prop to the waiter, who hurried off to hang it up and return with our rosé. Even in the diminished light of the alcove, Anne's sheer blouse was working its magic and I couldn't help but notice the waiter taking a few tentative looks at Anne's cleavage and bra visible through the material.

The rosé was beautifully chilled and we ordered a second bottle when the waiter brought our cous-cous and tagine. He lingered at my side (directly opposite my wife!) for several minutes to make sure we were happy with our dishes.

The food was delicious. We swapped and shared the two dishes and chatted and giggled our way through the second bottle of rosé. The waiter returned every so often to check on us, paying particular attention to Anne, of course.

Neither of us could face dessert, so we decided we'd pop into a café on the way home for an expresso and cognac.

Anne said she had to pay a visit to the ladies before we left and started to get up. As she rose from her seat I took her by the hand and said, "when you come back, make sure your bra is in your bag."

She immediately sat back down. "What?"

"You heard," I said, "make sure your bra is in your bag. Or, if you prefer, just bring it to me and I'll put it in my pocket." I retorted with a smile.

I could sense the confusion in her mind and was beginning to think she might already veto my request, when she just got up without a word and marched through the restaurant to the ladies hidden behind a draped curtain.

Our waiter was even too slow to catch her as she rushed past, but he stationed himself by the entrance in anticipation of her return, I presumed.

After 10 minutes I was beginning to get anxious, the waiter too had decided to return to his duties and left his post by the curtained entrance. I thought I ought to go check on her and got up to do just that, when I saw her appear through the curtain.

Without hesitation my eyes were drawn to her breasts. "Would I, or wouldn't I see them?" I thought.

I needn't have doubted her. Even across the restaurant I could see the outline of her nipples through the material. Anne walked proudly back to our table and quickly sat down. Her arms automatically moved into position to conceal herself from view.

"Satisfied?"

"Darling," I said, "I am so proud of you. You are unbelievable. Are you ready to go?"

As I said it, I called the waiter over to ask for the bill. He directed us to pay at the cashier and went to fetch Anne's Pashmina. As he was fetching it, ever the gentleman, I helped Anne out of her chair and walked behind her towards the cashier's desk.

As our waiter started to hand over the Pashmina, I intervened and said I would carry it for her and draped it over my arm. I then walked towards the door leaving Anne to pay for our meal, knowing full well she would have to lower her arms to reach for her money or credit card.

I stopped by the door and looked back. She was glaring at me, fully aware of my plan. She seemed to acquiesce quite quickly and gave up any attempts to cover herself. After paying, she brazenly strode towards the door with her arms by her side. I could see her breasts jiggling provocatively under her blouse. Our waiter was running after her, begging her to be sure to come again and to make sure she sat at his table.

Anne turned, gave the waiter an eyeful of her breasts and nipples and said that she would definitely be back, before grabbing my hand and pulling me through the door.

Our waiter stood watching and calling to us at the door until we turned the corner a good 200 yards down the street. As soon as we turned into the side street, Anne pushed me against the wall, stuck her tongue in my mouth and kissed me more passionately than she'd ever kissed me before - or so it seemed.

When she came up for breath, she huskily whispered, "Home. Now!" and set off walking, almost jogging, in the direction of the villa, her heels clicking sexily on the cobbles.

I followed on behind, keeping my distance, so I could watch the reactions from people strolling in the street. Anne kept looking back and urging me to get a move on.

I caught up with her as were about to reach the ring road that marks the end of the old town. I stopped her, kissed her again, then led her towards a small café.

"No," she said, "I really need to get back, I want you in me."

"Ok," I said, "but this means for two days you are not allowed to use a veto. You must do absolutely anything I say. Is that clear?"

She looked at me for a moment. "Anything? Absolutely anything?"

"That's right," I said, "that will be your punishment for disobeying me today."

I looked away from her eyes and down at her breasts and could clearly see her lovely brown areolae through her blouse. I wanted her now, as well.

"If that's what it takes, I agree, but let's go back now, please."

As a conciliatory gesture, I went to wrap the Pashmina around her, but she refused it.

"There's no need," she said, "I rather enjoy being ogled."

1-4. Net Result

We eventually fell asleep in the early hours after a torrid and passionate few hours. As we fell asleep Anne told me how shocked she had been by how aroused she had become after removing her bra and flaunting her C-cup breasts under her blouse.

I had reiterated how proud I had been of her and how sexy and beautiful she was. Neither of us mentioned that she had promised to do anything I commanded the following day, after I had allowed her to return home earlier than I had originally planned. She probably hoped I would forget about her promise.

I woke early the next morning, full of anticipation for the day. I left Anne sleeping naked in our bed. I started the coffee then popped out to the local *boulangerie* to pick up a couple of fresh baguettes and 4 hot croissants. When I got back the coffee was ready. I put the jam on the table and we now had everything we needed for a typical French breakfast on the veranda.

I tiptoed into the bedroom and snuggled next to my darling wife, kissing her on the neck. She stirred and turned to me offering a big smile.

"Breakfast on the veranda is ready," I said, jumping up. "No need to get dressed, come as you are."

Anne looked at me. "I'm totally naked, what will the neighbors think?"

❊ ❊ ❊

"Darling," I said, "for a start the neighbor can only see our veranda from his upstairs balcony, so I doubt whether that will happen at this time of day, and secondly, you have to do everything I say today without question, so I want your naked body on the veranda, now!"

"Yes, sir," she quipped jokingly and followed me onto the veranda, looking sheepishly up at the neighbor's balcony. Seeing no one there, she sat at the table.

It's strange how the fact she was naked outside made it so much more erotic than naked in the bedroom. I couldn't believe how turned on I was getting sitting opposite my naked wife. I was also hoping our neighbor might pop his head over the balcony, but that would have just been a bonus on this lovely, sunny day.

Seeing Anne in the sunlight her tan lines were quite stark. She had never been one for topless tanning even on holiday, so her breasts and bottom were rather white compared to the rest of her body. Although I find tan lines a turn on, I thought I should make time over the next 9 days (before my project started) for Anne to get an all over tan. But today we had other things to do to help prove to her that men find her attractive.

We lingered on the veranda sipping our coffees. I was in no rush to go back inside, because I wanted her to become more accustomed to being naked outside, even if it was only in our own backyard.

Eventually we went back into the bedroom and while Anne was in the shower, I picked out clothes for her to wear and got the camera ready. I also logged on to one of my favorite websites for sharing wife photos. I'd lurked on this site occasionally over the years, but I'd never mentioned the site to Anne, nor ever uploaded any photos of her. I was hoping to change this today.

Anne came out of the bathroom with her hair ready and a touch of make up with just a towel tied round her chest. She was a bit surprised when she saw the clothes, as they were the same as she had worn the previous evening. But she gave me a quick kiss then proceeded to dress. I had included the black balcony bra for starters. I'd soon be ditching it.

"Right," she said, turinng to me. "All ready. Where are we going?"

"Onto the veranda," I said, "That's all for the moment. Follow me."

We walked onto the veranda where I had set up a sun lounger in the shade ready as a prop for my photo-shoot.

"This morning, you are my model. I am going to take some hot and sexy pictures of you. All you have to do is be yourself."

I saw her look tentatively up at the neighboring balcony: still nobody there.

"Ok," she said, "Where do you want me?"

❁ ❁ ❁

I directed her first to stand by the wall and take some sexy poses. I wanted to capture her long legs, the curve of her breasts, the delightful swell of her cleavage and, if I could, the hint of nipple through the transparent bra and sheer blouse. I also took some shots from the rear to show of her lovely bum. I had her lean against the wall with her hands high, as if she was being frisked, and got a superb shot of the tops of her stocking peeping beneath her skirt. She then sat on the lounger and I took shots from above to beautifully capture her cleavage. She opened a couple of buttons more on her blouse to make her cleavage even more deep and enticing.

"Done for the moment," I said. "Come on in and relax, grab a drink and we'll continue in a little while."

"That was fun," Anne said. "Hopefully the pictures are worthwhile."

"Oh, they will be," I replied, "they definitely will be."

Anne went to the kitchen to fetch some drinks for us both. I went over to the computer I had put on the veranda table and started uploading the images from the camera. To my surprise I'd taken over 50 photos. As Anne returned with the drinks, I'd just loaded them into iPhoto so we could choose our favorites.

Anne sat next to me and gave me a peck on the cheek, as I started to scroll through the images of her. I'm not the world's best photographer, but even I was amazed at how sexy she looked. I'd failed miserably with some pictures, but there were a good dozen that were just what I was looking for - subtly sexy. Wow, what a woman I'd married.

Together we selected our top 10. Even Anne liked some of them and didn't make her normal derogatory comments about herself. "Progress," I thought, "real progress." Any of those that showed her face I cropped to make the picture anonymous.

"What are you doing?" she asked. "You can't tell it's me."

"Exactly," I said. "Now we can post them anonymously."

"Post them? Where?" she looked at me in panic.

"Don't worry. You said yourself, no one will know you. Today we're going to get the first tangible proof that other men find you hot." As I spoke I opened the website I'd selected and showed her how it worked. I opened some of the posts showing wives and girlfriends in various states of undress followed by comments from other members.

Anne was intrigued and wanted to see more. One photo posted showed a woman in the nude with her legs wide open. Anne recoiled with panic.

"No way," she said, "there's no way you're posting a picture of me like that."

"Calm down," I said, "who said anything about photos like that?

We're going to put up some of the photos we took just now and see the reaction. If our audience want more we'll show something a little more daring. Ok?"

Even before she could respond I had started a new thread and uploaded her first photo. Within seconds there was a comment: "Great start, let's see more."

"Let me see," Anne said, "what did he say".

Over the next 10 minutes or so I added half a dozen photos and Anne devoured all the comments. They were all extremely complimentary and most of them were asking to see more, just as I had anticipated.

"Come on" I said, "let's keep your fan club happy."

We went over to the wall where I'd taken the previous shots. This time I had her face the wall and bend to the waist and spread her legs. I love upskirt shots, and these were stunning. She then sat on the sun lounger and leaned forward with her knees spread. Delicious. You could see her cleavage almost to her nipples and her black thong and stocking tops. I was in raptures.

She didn't even demure when I told her to open her blouse and eventually she completely took it off. I took photos of her in her bra from various angles in various poses. The shots were tantalizing because her nipples were rock hard and partially visible through the transparent fabric of the bra. But I wanted more. I told her to get ready for the next shots while I uploaded some more photos. I wanted her in the blouse with no bra.

I gave her a sultry kiss then went over to the computer to select and upload some more photos. Comments had been pouring in while we were away and some were worried we had stopped posting because of the delay.

It only took me a few minutes to upload and I was back to capture even more sexy photos of my lovely wife. As she leaned back against the wall in her sheer blouse, short skirt and heels I was rock hard. Her nipples were poking through the material and you could clearly see her dark brown areolae. I took a pile of photos from all angles and had her undo the buttons on the blouse one by one until it hung open revealing the inner curves of her breasts.

As she bent forward the blouse parted to reveal the whole of her breasts. Anne had been surprisingly silent during the shoot and said nothing even as I took these last shots showing all her breasts. I moved across to her and kissed her on the lips. As I did so, I tweaked her nipples. She moaned with lust.

I slipped her blouse from her shoulders and down her arms. She was now totally topless. I had her resume the bent pose with her hands against the wall and then put my hands up her skirt and pulled her thong off and dropped it behind me. I took several photos with her legs together. From the slight angle I was standing at, one swinging breast was beautifully visible, as was a peek of her pussy.

"Spread your legs", I said.

She submissively did as requested, knowing full well that I had a spectacular view of her pussy lips. She didn't shave her pubes, merely trimmed them, so the pussy wasn't as fully displayed as it would be shaved. When I'd taken a few dozen photos from the rear, I went and hugged her from behind. Pulling her to an upright position and grabbing both breasts as I did. She turned her head to kiss me and I knew she was hot and ready for the next step.

I took hold of her skirt and undid the zipper at the back and dropped it down. She obediently stepped out of it.

Now I had her pose with her back to the wall and picked up the camera again.

She did some demure shots trying to cover her breasts and pussy with her hands, but soon she was brazenly posing like a professional. My brain was buzzing. What had I done? Could this be my once demure wife posing like a glamour model?

My cock was loving it, my brain was in overdrive.

After I've no idea how many photos, I led her to the sun lounger. The back of the lounger was slightly raised, so she was sitting partially upright when she leaned back. She put her arms behind her head and pulled her knees up. Her breasts were perfect. Her nipples were pointing directly at the camera.

❊ ❊ ❊

I now opened her legs slightly with my hand and took some more shots. Her pussy was still hidden in the shadows of her thighs. I pushed them open some more, then more and eventually with her legs bent her knees were pointing outwards and her sopping wet pussy was invitingly and brazenly wide open for everyone to see. My hands were trembling as I took photo after photo. I had Anne put a finger in her mouth, tweak her nipples and when I saw how excited she was becoming, told her in a firm voice to bring herself to orgasm and carried on taking photos as if it was the most natural thing in the world.

Without saying a word, her hand moved slowly down her stomach and finally her middle finger slipped sloppily between her pussy lips. Her eyes were glazed and her finger moved smoothly in and out. Low moans were coming from her throat. I kept forgetting to take any photos, I was so enraptured. As her orgasm neared, her fingers moved over her clitoris more and more. The nearer her orgasm came, the more frenzied her movements. As her orgasm shuddered through her body, I made sure I got full body pictures, close ups of her pussy and fingers and shots of her orgasmic face. This was so intense I was close to cumming myself. My boxers were probably soaked in pre-cum.

As Anne's orgasm subsided I put the camera down and took her in my arms. I couldn't believe what she had done this morning. I held her tightly and told her how much I loved her.

I asked her if she wanted a robe, but she refused it, choosing to stay naked as we both sat down at the computer.

❁ ❁ ❁

In just over an hour I had taken almost 300 explicit photos of my wanton wife. I was in ecstasy and tremblingly loaded all the latest shots onto the computer. Comments had been piling up about our earlier postings. Anne fetched her iPad and logged on to the site to read the comments more closely.

She began to type furiously and I guessed she was answering her fans personally.

I selected my favorite photos from the latest batch and cropped them suitably before posting them teasingly one by one on Anne's thread. Purposely, I didn't ask Anne which she preferred - I wanted to make sure she didn't stop me posting some of the later more explicit shots. Even though she seemed to be experiencing a real high at the moment, the realization that explicit shots were being uploaded for all the world to see, even anonymously, might bring her out of her euphoria.

As of yet, Anne had only shown her cleavage and stocking tops in her posts. The next shot I uploaded was of her without a bra. The fullness of her breasts and her nipples were clearly visible.

The response on the site was immediate. Anne actually blushed at one man's comment and began typing furiously again.

For the next hour I uploaded Anne's photos every 3-4 minutes or so. Each photo was more daring than the next. Anne was intrigued by the number of men who wanted to chat on cam, but so far she had refused them all. Other men (and to Anne's surprise, women too) were making requests for particular types of photo: tits hanging, shaved, full frontal, full face and the like. Anne was taking it all very calmly sitting naked on our veranda. She said she felt safe behind her anonymity in the photos and wasn't sure if she could ever do this with her face revealed. The more photos I put and the more Anne added her responses to comments, the more comments seemed to appear.

Finally, after numerous requests, I posted a full frontal. Anne gasped when she saw it. The positive comments soon kept her busy. The upskirt with no panties was very popular, and even more so the upskirt, no panties with legs spread. Anne's popularity was confirmed when her post was labelled the "hot post of the day".

When the photo of Anne sitting naked on the sun lounger with her knees up appeared, I could feel the tension in Anne. She knew what was coming. So far, she hadn't made one remark to me about any of the images, she was so intent on the comments.

I waited a few minutes before posting the next with her pussy hiding in the shadows of her thighs. I loved the shot, an absolute tease.

Her fans were clamoring for her to open her legs wide. I couldn't deny them and with my cock straining to be released, I posted Anne totally naked with her legs spread. Her pussy lips were glistening with wetness, her arms were folded behind her head and she was looking defiantly at the camera.

"Oh, shit!" I thought, "I forgot to crop the photo." There was no way I could stop it being posted now.

I waited for Anne to react. When she put down her iPad and turned to me, I was ready for the worse.

"Are you going to fuck me today?" she asked spreading her legs over the arms of the chair so I could see how wet and ready she was. I had never heard her use such language.

I said nothing, I just knelt down in front of her and began to lick and finger fuck her pussy. She exploded within a minute.

"Now put on your skirt, blouse and heels, we're going for a late lunch and a drink in town." I said in my most commanding voice.

As she went to collect her clothes, I saw what her last comment had been: "Thank you for all your lovely comments. I'll post again soon. Now my pussy's on fire and I'm going to fuck my man xxxxx."

All I could do was smile. What an exhibitionist I had created. "I have to enjoy this while it lasts", I thought to myself.

Anne came back out dressed. Her bra was missing as requested, her breasts jiggling seductively and her nipples fully visible under the white blouse.

"Turn round and bend over," I commanded trying to hold back

my smile, "with your legs spread."

She bent slowly at the waist, looking back at me as she did.

Bingo. Her hairy pussy was in full view. She smirked at me as I discovered she had followed my instructions.

"See anything you like?" she quipped as she stood back up and smoothed down her skirt.

"More than you can imagine, my darling," I answered, wondering how long I could deny myself.

"Let's go," I said, "we have to be back in time for our neighbor. Remember? You invited him over for drinks."

"Should we go put him off?" she asked.

"No, I don't think we should. I'm sure he'll enjoy his visit," I said with a saucy wink.

Anne laughed and we set off for the town. I picked up my trusty camera on the way out and rearranged my trousers to make it easier to walk.

PART TWO

Wife Laid Bare

2-1. Invitation

The last 24 hours had been the most erotic of our married life. After a week in Provence in the south of France, I had begun to enjoy the fantasy of showing off my wife in real life. To my surprise and absolute delight, Anne, my once shy, but sexy wife, pushing 40 and oftentimes unsure about her own body, was blooming.

We had got back to our villa on the northern periphery of Aix en Provence late last night. The evening had been a first for both of us, when Anne, at my request, had worn a sheer blouse over a black bra and, later in the evening in the restaurant, had removed it to reveal her breasts and big brown areolae to the world. All the way back to our villa, her jiggling breasts were stunningly visible under her blouse. Not only did this arouse me, but Anne was desperate to feel my cock in her pussy the moment we stepped through the door. And then, this morning, we had posted revealing shots of Anne on an amateur site. Within hours Anne had a huge fan club of avid voyeurs.

It was about 5:30 when we got back to the villa after our trip into Aix that afternoon. Anne had visibly enjoyed titilating the men of the town by going braless with a sheer white blouse.

The afternoon had been more erotic than I could have ever imagined. I had taken any number of pictures all over Aix of Anne posing. She had no problem letting me take revealing upskirt shots whenever I asked.

I was enthralled by her tits as they quivered visibly under her blouse as she walked. As to be expected Anne was very popular in the cafés we visited and we always had the most attentive service. Numerous men made comments to her as she passed, whereas some women were not so complimentary. Anne just smiled sweetly. We also paid a visit to her favorite jewelry shop, ostensibly to buy her a gift, but really I just wanted to see the young assistant's eyes when she entered the shop. I wasn't disappointed. The poor boy almost came in his pants when Anne greeted him cheerily and asked about a piece of jewelry in the window. She tried on several necklaces, always asking the boy to fasten them and asking his opinion, so that he had to look at her neck and chest. She was really enjoying the attention. I was more than enjoying it too.

Unfortunately I couldn't jump straight into bed with her when we got back, because the previous evening Anne had spontaneously chosen to invite our neighbor over for drinks. We'd told Antoine, the neighbor, to pop by about 6, so we only had half an hour or so to set out some nibbles and tidy up a bit.

Anne had seemingly forgotten that she had no bra and no panties on as she rushed around tidying and preparing the nibbles. My cunning plan to get back as late as possible had apparently worked.

Just after 6 the doorbell rang.

"Can you get it," I shouted from the bathroom, "I'm a bit tied up."

I heard Anne's heels clacking along the hallway. I followed behind. I didn't want to miss Antoine's face when Anne opened the door.

I saw Antoine do a double take and then collected himself, "Good evening, Anne, you look ravishing," he said as he stepped through the door and kissed her on the cheek 4 times, as they do in this part of France. He hardly noticed me as I stood further down the hallway. He and Anne were chatting away. Antoine touched her several times on the arm and as they turned to walk towards me, he put his hand on the small of her back.

I couldn't help the pangs of jealousy, but I was even more aroused by Antoine's attentions to Anne.

Antoine and I shook hands and I led the way to the veranda. I directed Antoine to one of the armchairs and motioned Anne to sit on the other one opposite and I went to fetch our aperitifs.

When I returned they were chatting away like old friends. They hardly noticed as I handed them their glasses. I sat to one side watching them. I just loved the way my darling's breasts swayed and bounced in her blouse as she talked animatedly. Her nipples were poking through the material even more than earlier, so I guessed she was enjoying Antoine's visit. Her long legs were crossed and she was leaning forward listening intently to what our guest had to say.

❀ ❀ ❀

Antoine was asking how we liked the villa and Aix. Anne said she found the whole place thrilling and winked at me. We talked about my project and how long we'd be here and Antoine ascertained that Anne would have plenty of free time during the day while I was busy.

She agreed that she would, but that she had plans and would not be bored.

"I think," Antoine mused, "a woman of your beauty and style might be interested in a private club I am proud to be a member of, here in Aix."

"A private club? What kind of club?" Anne shifted forward in her chair and uncrossed and crossed her legs.

"It's an exclusive club, membership is by invitation alone, primarily for gentlemen. However, ladies who pass a stringent entrance test are eligible to be honorary members. We only meet a few times a month, but I think you would thoroughly enjoy our sessions. Naturally, your husband," Antoine looked at me for just about the first time that evening, "would also become an honorary member with you."

Anne didn't even look my way, as she asked, "so, do you think I would pass the test?"

"Absolutely," said Antoine, "I have no doubt you would pass with flying colors. If you like, I could arrange a test for this week, shall we say the day after tomorrow?"

❋ ❋ ❋

"Well, I suppose so… where does it take place? And who carries out the test?" she enquired enthusiastically.

I started to say something, but Antoine, interjected before I could go on.

"The club's supreme master is the only one allowed to perform the test. I will ask him to come here at 7 p.m. on Thursday. Your husband will receive a note in advance with instructions on how to proceed. I think you will both be very pleased you decided to become honorary members."

Before we had time to say much else, Antoine was excusing himself and wishing us a good evening. He said we would receive the instructions on Thursday morning and that we should take them very seriously, as there was only one chance. If Anne failed this, she would never have another chance.

Antoine shook my hand warmly and Anne walked him to the door. As I was carrying the glasses back to the kitchen I saw him kiss Anne goodbye and then whisper something in her ear. As he did so, she stepped back in shock. "Oh, God," she said.

"I very much appreciated it, my dear," said Antoine, and stepped out closing the door behind him.

Anne came back into the kitchen looking distraught.

"Oh, shit no, no. I can't believe it."

※ ※ ※

"What is it?" I asked, feeling somewhat concerned.

"Today, on the veranda. Antoine saw it all. He was watching us, watching me, he saw me touch myself. He saw me orgasm. Oh, God."

"Well, what did he say to you? I doubt he's complaining. He wouldn't have come here tonight otherwise. He wouldn't have invited us to join his exclusive club, would he? He's probably gone back right now to wank himself to sleep dreaming of your body."

"Don't say that, Matt. I'm feeling mortified."

"But, it's true, you know. What do you think all those men on the site were doing today as they looked at your pictures? I bet you most of them made themselves cum at some point during your post. You made a lot of men very happy today - including me. One of them happened to be next door, but he appreciates your body in the way many men do. You are beautiful, sexy and eminently fuckable and I think you're beginning to grasp the effect you have on men as a whole. So stop worrying, and get in the bedroom. I've been saving myself all day for you."

2-2. Beach Revels

It was mid morning in our villa in Aix en Provence. After a simple French breakfast on the veranda, Anne had said she wanted to touch up her tan, so I suggested a day at the beach. She jumped at the idea. It only took her 10 minutes to be ready and waiting for me at the door.

"Come on slowcoach," she shouted to me in the kitchen. I was still stuffing the picnic cooler with wine and packing the camera in its bag.

Anne had put on a simple halter top, no bra and a flared skirt. Just flats today, heels aren't the best footwear for the beach. She kissed me before we pulled out of the driveway and told me how much she loved me.

Aix en Provence is situated in the hills above Marseille, so the nearest coastline is about 18 miles away, but the nearest beach is a good 25 miles away. But today we were on our way to the Camargue, about 80 miles to the west of Aix. We had been before to some of the stunning beaches. They beaches usually had sand dunes, few people and miles of sand.

We stopped in Arles for a quick coffee and snack then headed for the coast. My company had provided a Volkswagen Beetle soft-top, so we were enjoying the breeze in our hair as we zipped along the back roads through the Camargue National Park. Anne, as ever, was in a wonderful mood and was thrilled to be the first of us to see some of the famous white horses.

※ ※ ※

There are a pick of beaches here, but we chose one just past the salt flats with their eery mounds of salt because we liked the dunes it offers. In the summer months, there can be a fair amount of people, but at this time of year, they were dotted here and there on the beach and no doubt there were some hidden amongst the dunes.

We saw a few couples as we tramped through the dunes, but there was plenty of space for everyone to have some privacy. We eventually chose a cosy spot protected from the wind blowing in from the sea and sheltered from other sun worshippers.

I said nothing when Anne put on her bikini, but was feeling a tad disappointed that she hadn't wanted to go at least topless. She had suddenly become shy again after 2 days of exhibitionism. The only people nearby were a couple beyond the next dune. We had seen them as we walked past. Both were lying on their stomachs totally naked and hardly stirred as we traipsed by.

I changed into my swimming trunks and then we spread out our towels. Anne proceeded to lie face down. I sat up and chose to read a book on my iPad using one of the inflatable back rests we had brought with us. Before I started reading, I offered Anne some sun screen. She mumbled assent, so I began rubbing it liberally over the back of her legs. When I reached her back I undid the strap of her bikini top and covered her back and shoulders in the oil, making sure she was totally protected.

As of yet I hadn't reminded Anne that she was still under the 48 hour obligation to do all I required. I decided to see how things progressed.

After an hour or so, Anne decided to turn over and started to fasten the clasp. I put out my hand to stop her and told her it was time to get some sun on her breasts. She acquiesced with a slight sigh and stuffed the bikini top in her bag, put on her sunglasses and lay back down on the towel on her back.

"What about the sun screen?" I asked. "Do you want me to put some on you?"

"No, it's ok, I'll do it," she said, and proceeded to slop the thick cream on her legs, stomach and then over her breasts, before dabbing some on her face.

I watched entranced as ever. There's nothing sexier than a woman rubbing sun oil onto her own body.

As the sun hit its zenith, it was very hot. Lying on the towel on her back, Anne's body was glistening from the sun. Every once in a while she would shift her legs or run her fingers along the edge of her string bikini to wipe away some of the perspiration that gathered there.

At one point a couple of young guys of about 19 or 20 walked past us on the way to the beach. They nodded to me and took a keen interest in my wife's assets - much to my pleasure. They were both totally naked and I was quick to notice that one of them had a sizeable dick, even as it hung limply.

※ ※ ※

About 5 minutes later the same two went back in the other direction and lingered a good while to have a good look at my wife. I pretended to be absorbed in my book and only watched them out of the corner of my eye. They made some comments about her nipples, I think, but they spoke too softly for me to hear properly.

Instead of continuing across the next sand dune, the two sat down about 15 yards from Anne and me looking in our direction.

I whispered to Anne, all the while pretending to be absorbed in my book, "There are a couple of young men watching you. They seem fascinated by your body. Don't move yet."

Her eyes widened under her sunglasses. I know she had begun to enjoy men ogling her after yesterday, so I hoped she would rise to the challenge today as well. Until two days ago, although she has a lovely body, but she had still felt very shy about being exposed or vulnerable. I felt she had a body of a woman 10 years younger than her age. It amazed me how often men followed her with their eyes when she walked down the street.

"What you're going to do," I said, "is just take some of your tanning oil and apply it to your body, nice and slowly. Sexily."

She looked at me as if I was crazy, then smiled shaking her head, and leaned over on her elbow to get the tanning oil from her bag. She pulled the back support behind her and sat up without looking directly in the direction of the two men. I put on my dark sunglasses too, so I could follow what was happening surreptitiously, and continued as if reading my book.

There was no question they were intently watching my sexy wife.

As I looked to the side, I could see her applying the tanning oil slowly and seductively, just like I wanted. She poured some oil into her palm, then reached down to her ankles and slowly massaged it in, moving inch by inch up her legs. Her breasts were jiggling sexily as she moved forwards and back. She bent her legs to apply oil to her inner thigh. First one, then the other.

When her legs were done, she poured a line of oil along her arms and spread it over her shoulders. She now dribbled some oil onto each breast, She massaged the oil lovingly into her soft breasts, but also treating them quite roughly it seemed, pushing her fingers into them. Then she lay back and spread more of the oil on her stomach.

As I watched her, my hard on grew. At this point I looked up, and saw that neither young man was soft any more. Their hard ons were clearly visible even from this distance. I whispered to Anne that she was having an obvious effect on the two young men and that one of them had a very impressive cock.

"They're both totally naked," and quickly added, "But, don't look yet."

She was still sliding the oil down across her stomach, past her pretty navel and down to the edge of her small bikini bottoms.

I looked up and was quite amazed to see that both young men were openly caressing their cocks.

I knelt down beside her. I was rock hard, seeing my wife applying the oil and seeing the young men so aroused only 15 yards away. I knew I would find it exciting, but this was unbelievable.

Anne moved her head and looked at me.

"How was that?" she said.

I picked up the bottle of tanning oil. "Turn over, my darling. They both have big hard ons and they are watching your every move. How do you feel?"

"Weird."

"You look so hot."

She smiled. "I feel hot."

Her bikini bottom was a thong that left absolutely nothing to the imagination.

"You have a delicious bottom," I said as she hesitated.

When she was once more lying on her tummy, I poured some oil onto her back and rubbed it in gently. She put her head on her hands and seemed to relax a little.

"How does it feel having me spread oil on your body while two men are watching you? You realize they are touching themselves now?"

Anne just purred and said and nothing else.

I was finding this so erotic that I was little peeved she didn't say more.

"They're still there. They love your oiled body. You've really make them hard, how does that make you feel?"

She just purred in her throat again, a little deeper and a little longer this time. I now moved down to her legs applying the oil along her toned calves, then her thighs, right up to the cheeks of her delicious bottom. I poured more oil onto her cheeks and kneaded it in.

"Mmm," she sighed and opened her legs just a little. I slid my hands back down to her knees and then up along the inside of her thighs. As I reached her thong I spotted the wetness in the crotch of her thin bikini bottom. She was very aroused! I kept rubbing on the oil.

"Yes, they're still watching, they've actually moved closer. They are both stroking their dicks openly now, looking at you and stroking."

My sexy wife spread her legs a little wider and I could see the swell of her pussy lips outlined through the stretched bikini bottom.

"I'm sure they enjoyed watching your fingers caressing your soft skin, touching your breasts, caressing your stomach. I bet you could almost feel their eyes on you."

"Mmmm yes," she murmured as she started to shift her hips slightly, lifting them almost imperceptibly.

I now slid my hands up inside her thigh and let my finger caress her pussy softly. My dick was leaking pre-cum copiously.

I continued to knead her bare bottom some more and smiled as she spread her legs wider. The two guys were getting quite a show.

"Yes," I whispered, "they have come closer. They are standing now with their dicks in their hands, rubbing furiously. I bet they want to grab hold of your lovely breasts and bite your nipples and tug on them with their teeth. What would that feel like with two of them playing with your tits at once?

"Oh God!" she said. She raised her bottom slightly and began moving it around. I slid my hand along her bum crack, tracing the material of her thong. I felt like ramming my dick into her pussy there and then.

❊ ❊ ❊

"You know, I bet the one with the huge dick wants to slide his hand over your ass and pull down your bikini bottom." As I spoke I pulled down her thong just to the bottom of her buttocks. "so he can slide his dick across your lovely bum cheeks before sliding it along your hot, wet slit."

This time she groaned and she lifted lift her ass even more. Her eyes were closed, she was biting her lip. I leaned over and whispered to her.

"Now, my darling, turn over. When you turn over put some more oil on your breasts and tease your nipples. That will send them right over the edge."

She opened her eyes. "Okay," was all she said. He breathing was heavy and her skin was glowing with the oil. She was very aroused.

I sat back on my towel and looked at the young men. The one with the huge dick was stroking slowly. His dick bent upwards and the head of his dick was red and very bulbous. The other one had a smaller dick and was rubbing quite fast. They were moving cautiously forward. They were now about 5 steps from my wife's delights.

She turned over as they approached. She hadn't bothered to pull up her bikini bottom. She was so erotic. I could see the top of the pubic hair on her mound. Once again she began spreading the oil on her breasts, massaging them, tugging on her nipples and twisting them. Her breasts were fabulous, full and firm, with tight hard nipples. Her tummy was rising and falling. She pulled her knees up slightly then put them down again. She was so wonderful, so amazing. She was moaning to herself as if in a trance.

What happened next made me grab my own dick it was so erotic.

She slid her fingers slowly down her tummy, digging them into her oily skin, inching their way down to her pussy. She dropped both legs flat on the towel and slid her fingers under her bikini bottom. She was fingering herself in full view of the guys! I wanted to come right then!

Then she opened her legs and slipped her bikini bottom out of the way. Even from the side I could clearly see the wet pink folds of her pussy lips.

Suddenly, with all eyes on her pussy lips, she took off her sunglasses and looked directly at the young men stroking themselves. She smiled and motioned to them to move forward. The men initially stopped in their tracks, but when they saw her hand beckoning them closer, they slowly moved forward coming to the edge of Anne's towel staring down at her luscious pussy. Both dicks looked thick and bulbous from so close.

I was rooted to the spot, sitting on my towel, mesmerized by the two strange dicks. By now my wife's fingers were moving up and down her slit, sinking into her pussy and sliding up over her clit.

As the men resumed their stroking she moaned out loud. Her hips were bucking as she smiled up at them, moving her fingers over and around her clit, and using her other hand to massage her breast and pull her nipple hard.

Then it happened. The young man with the smaller dick uttered a very brief moan and then he came. He shot long arcs of sperm onto Anne's legs and towel. Long white threads of cum fell onto her. As the spunk hit her legs she began thrashing about. She was screaming now as she bucked against her glistening fingers. The second young man had moved even closer and he now shot thick wads of cum that landed on Anne's leg, hand and tummy. As the warm spunk hit her body and the young man grunted in orgasm Anne shuddered with her own shuddering orgasm. She was rubbing her fingers rapidly over her clit until finally she slowed and just let her fingers slip along her slit.

I just stared in amazement at her for at least thirty more seconds. Then we both looked up at the young men, but they were already retreating over the dune.

She looked at me as I stood up and released my own dick from my trunks, thick, ripe and ready. "Oh God," she said, and started to finger herself again. This was too much for me. In a few seconds I shot my load. Beautiful globs of thick cum splashed onto my wife. At the same time, she came again, thrashing, twisting: a long and intense orgasm.

I sunk onto my knees next to her and kissed her soft lips. She pulled me fiercely to her and ravaged my tongue with hers. When the kiss was over she pulled away and smiled.

"Was that hot or what?" she said. "Have you noticed my hand, leg and belly are covered in cum?"

As she said it she scooped up a dollop with her index finger. She studied it for a moment and then stuck her finger in her mouth and sucked it clean.

"Mmm," she cooed, "what about a creamy kiss?" She pulled me too her and stuck her tongue in my mouth. I could taste the salty spunk on her tongue. Too my surprise I was getting aroused again. The thought of tasting another man's thick cum was unbelievably sexy. I kissed her avidly and dipped my own fingers in the white goo on her tummy. She licked it from my fingers seductively and I locked lips with her again.

She pulled away and said abruptly, "I think we should start to head back, so we can relive today lying in our own bed. What do you reckon?"

How could I refuse? My mind was already full of vivid images of bulbous cocks, thick white spunk, soft wet pussy lips and the taste of another man's cum. I would relive it eternally.

2-3. Arles

As we were driving into Arles, Anne saw a sign for a dance party that evening in the town. Anne loves dancing and rarely gets the chance as I feel so inadequate on the dance floor.

"Please…" she pleaded. "We could stay over in a hotel and make a night of it. What do you think?"

I looked a bit skeptical at the idea.

"I won't wear any panties all night, if we can stay. Or bra, for that matter, as I don't have one with me."

How could I refuse. Also, the thought of watching my pantyless wife dancing with some hunky locals had my brain go into overdrive.

Within minutes we found out where the dance venue was and were pleased to discover it was next door to a decent-looking 4 star hotel.

"Are you sure about this?" I asked.

"Are you? Do you want to let your sexy wife loose on the local studs?"

That settled it, we parked the car and with our beach bag and picnic basket checked in to the best room they had.

❈ ❈ ❈

The dance didn't start for a couple of hours, so I suggested we hit the town, get Anne a new party dress and have a bite to eat and take a look at the roman amphitheater while we were here. Anne readily agreed and we strolled into the town centre. The first shop we saw was a decent-looking boutique with some sexy dresses in the window. We went in and Anne started to comb through the racks.

I was more intrigued by the lingerie department. While Anne went to try on some dresses she'd found, I quickly purchased her a delightfully daring sheer babydoll with matching panties. The package was miniscule, so it fit easily into my pocket.

Anne appeared from the cubicle in a midi-length flowery number. It didn't do anything for me, or her figure. After about 10 dresses, I was becoming exasperated, so she told me to go to the bar across the street and she would follow me soon, when she had decided herself.

Not one to argue, I went and sat at a table on the terrace and ordered a beer.

45 minutes and 2 beers later my darling wife appeared by my side. She was carrying a large carrier bag in one hand, so I knew she had found something. She wouldn't let me look, it was to be a surprise.

Time was running short for the amphitheater, so we decided to give it a miss this time and ordered the meal of the day from the bar I'd been in for almost an hour.

As ever a quick meal in France took about an hour and a half, but we reckoned we'd arrive at the dance as it was getting warmed up.

Back at the hotel Anne grabbed the bathroom and spent a good while preparing herself.

When she came out I realised it had been time well spent. She looked stunning. The dress was lilac in colour with a deep v-neckline almost to her navel with cross straps over the bust to hold it in place. The main dress came down to just below her buttocks from where a flowing sheer skirt came down to her ankles. Her breasts were on display and when she danced the skirt would fly in all directions revealing her thighs and much more. She had made a superb choice.

As I admired her she turned, spread her legs and bent at the waist. She had kept her promise and the sight of her hairy pussy made me rock hard in a second.

We got to the dance about an hour after it had started. The place was empty. The music was dire. We got a couple of drinks and chose one of the numerous empty tables close to the almost empty dancefloor. The youngest "stud" in the place would have been 60 and all the men we saw were dancing with wives of a similar age. Anne was heartbroken. The excitement of the day was rapidly evaporating.

I told her to drink up and grabbed her hand. I walked her back to the hotel and into the lift, when she finally spoke.

"What are you doing?"

"Plan B," I said, "We are going to have a night to remember."

She looked at me quizzically, but said nothing.

Back in the room, I kissed her gently and handed her the gift I had bought in the shop.

"Go put this on," I said, "And trust me, tonight will be special."

She came out of the bathroom in the babydoll and matching panties a few minutes later.

"Will I do?" she whispered huskily.

I was speechless. There's something about sheer material that drives me wild. The babydoll was a very pale pink, tied at the front with a ribbon. The shoulder straps could be worn off-shoulder, just like Anne had them now. She knows her bare shoulders drive me wild. The folds of the babydoll came down to just over the sheer panties. I could make out her breasts through the sheer material, but they weren't clearly on display.

"Tantalisingly erotic," was my first thought, "I want to give this woman more pleasure than she's ever had," was my second.

"Come here," I said.

❄ ❄ ❄

She moved closer. I put my arms up and instead of hugging her as she expected, I tied a blindfold over her eyes. She gulped in shock, but was laughing as I guided her to lie down on the bed.

I began moving my fingers lightly over her thighs, up across her tummy and breasts to her neck and shoulders. Then I massaged her left arm gently and as I reached the wrist, much to her surprise tied a soft rope around it. I then did the same to her right wrist and tied her to the bed. She smiled as I kissed her on the lips and I then massaged my way down to her feet. She probably expected me to tie her feet too, but for the moment I left them free.

She was now firmly tied to the bed by her wrists. With her knees up and legs slightly apart I could just make out her pussy lips swelling through her delicious blonde bush under her panties. Under her babydoll, her areolae were big and brown and her nipples were enlarged and ready for my tongue and mouth. As yet she had only said three words since we came back into the room. She just smiled in my direction as I moved up to her face. I kissed her on the lips and pushed my tongue deep inside her inviting mouth.

"So," I said, "now it's time to go further with a fantasy that"'s been bubbling inside me for a while. "You looked so sexy tonight and I was ready to explode when you did as I asked and wore your panties. You really are special".

I kissed her again, knowing full well that she was probably feeling a little apprehensive about what this fantasy of mine might be. Over the years we'd revealed so many sexy and erotic thoughts to each other, this could be one of many options.

"Comfortable?" I asked. She nodded and lifted her head to kiss me once more on the lips. I looked at her beautiful body as I picked up the phone and called room service: "a bottle of chilled sweet white wine," I said into the phone.

I kissed my darling again and then to surprise her poured some massage oil onto one foot and then the other. She jumped in surprise at the first drops, but moaned with pleasure as I began spreading the oil liberally over her feet and legs. As I moved up her left leg, I poured more oil over her thigh and began gently rubbing it over her skin, careful not to touch her pussy.

As I massaged the oil into her thigh she let out a soft moan, but tensed as there was a knock at the door and we heard a voice say, "Room service".

"Shall I continue?" I asked. "Yes," she whispered in reply.

"Come in," I called.

A few seconds later the young waiter we'd seen in the hotel earlier in the day opened the door and stepped into the room holding a silver tray with a bottle of my darling's favorite wine and two wine glasses. He first saw me sitting on the bed and then did a double take as he realized there was a half-naked woman also on the bed. His eyes fell immediately upon her breasts, then pussy and no doubt he saw the outline of her pussy lips pink and pouting through her transparent panties.

"Just put it on the bedside table," I said nonchalantly, pointing to the table by the bed, all the time my heart beating like a steam-hammer in my chest. I continued to smooth the oil into my Anne's thigh as the young man walked in a trance to the bedside table and put down the tray. My wife hadn't moved since he came into the room, but I could see a slight flush on her chest and face.

"She's beautiful, isn't she?" I said, looking at the young man, who quickly looked away as I looked over at him. "Yes, yes, she is," he stammered.

"Would you like to watch while I give her a massage? Just sit on that chair," I said, pointing to the chair I had placed ready at the side of the bed with a perfect view of my Ann'es pussy, not really giving him an excuse to say no.

I noticed the bulge in his pants as he sat down and begin more boldly to take in my wife's body. I watched as his gaze moved up from her pussy to her breasts and her stiff nipples partly visible through her babydoll.

His eyes followed my hands as I moved down her leg and poured oil over her feet and began massaging it in. I splashed the oil liberally over her calves and made her legs glisten as I rubbed and smoothed each leg in turn. The young man watched intently as I moved my hands up over the knee on one leg and started massaging oil into my wife's thigh. She let out an occasional moan as I stroked her inner thigh and approached her swollen pussy.

I handed the oil bottle to the young man and pointed to the thigh on his side of the bed. He looked at me for a second, but quickly took the bottle and poured oil onto my wife's skin and began tentatively rubbing her thigh.

At the moment my wife had no idea that it wasn't me massaging her leg. I had gone slightly further more quickly than I had anticipated, but revealing my sexy wife to a stranger had made me feel so desirous of the beautiful woman lying so serenely on the bed. I wanted her to get extra pleasure for having fulfilled this fantasy of mine and I thought that a four-handed massage would make her feel even more special.

❖ ❖ ❖

The young man was vigorously rubbing my wife's leg. He moved down to her foot and then back up above the knee and over her thigh. He stopped just short of her pussy, but I watched his eyes lingering on her partly visible wet pussy lips. I longed to touch them and see how wet they were (as he probably did too), but decided to wait just a little longer. I indicated the other leg to the young man and he proceeded to massage it from foot to thigh, just like before, lingering at the top of her thigh. My wife was lying quite still, but gentle sighs and moans were coming from her every so often.

I asked her if everything was ok, and she just sighed with pleasure.

When the young man had reached the top of the thigh once more I motioned him to sit down again. I kissed my wife on the lips and said, shall we take a look at your beautiful breasts? She just moaned again softly and i looked across at the young man. "Would you like to have a look?", I said.

He managed to stammer out a yes and wriggled in the chair to accommodate his erection.

I was shaking as I asked if he'd like to undo the ribbon holding the top of the babydoll. He needed no encouragement. He moved closer to the bed quickly undid it. Once open, he pulled back the babydoll from both breasts, allowing himself to get a proper look. I watched his eyes widen as the soft material fell to the side to reveal her 36C breasts.

Her nipples were even bigger than usual. I picked up the oil bottle and began pouring oil over her nipples. It trickled down her breasts and onto her tummy. The young man looked at me imploringly and I just nodded. He placed a hand on both sides of her tummy before slipping through the oil up and over her breasts and nipples. The gasp of delight from my wife was deep and sexy. Her head went back and she moaned again. The young man was now intently playing with both nipples. I was watching entranced wondering just how far this would go.

I moved up the bed and kissed my wife on the lips. She responded hungrily and our tongues locked. All the time the nipple massage continued. I'm not sure if she had an inkling yet that it wasn't my hands making her moan in pleasure, but I don't think she really cared.

As I pulled away, I said I thought it was time to free her pussy from her panties. The young man looked at me and stopped massaging my wife's delicious nipples. I told him to stand at the foot of the bed, so he could get the best view. "Would you like to remove her panties?" I asked. I saw my wife stiffen at my words, so I moved up to give her another passionate kiss and told our guest to pull her panties off.

He didn't hesitate. Her knees were up and her legs slightly closed, so he leaned over her knees and took hold of both sides of the panties and pulled them slowly up to her knees then down to her feet and off. He immediately sniffed them and then to my surprise stuffed the panties in his pocket.

At the moment my wife's pussy was temptingly hidden in the shadows of her thighs. Now came for me one of the most erotic things I have ever witnessed. I told my darling to slowly open her legs. In that moment, I looked down at her with her arms tied to the bed, her beautiful breasts and dark brown nipples glistening with massage oil and then looked over to the young man who was standing transfixed at the foot of the bed. His bulge was impressive. I looked at my wife and could see tufts of blonde pubes between her legs and watched in awe as she slowly spread her thighs to reveal her engorged, pink, wet pussy lips to this stranger. The waiter and I were both entranced. I moved next to him at the foot of the bed and took in the superb view he had of my wife's luscious pussy, fully exposed with her thighs splayed wide.

"So," I said to my darling, my voice trembling with desire and lust, "would you like me to begin by sucking your nipples or caressing your pussy?"

"My nipples, my nipples", she replied with a moan.

"I think that's exactly what our new friend wanted too," I said, "that means he gets to caress your pussy."

My wife gasped as I said this and her legs involuntarily closed, but I took hold of her knees and pulled them apart. The young man knelt between them on the bed, looked at me and, as I nodded, he put a hand on each of her thighs. She tensed, but as he moved his hands towards her pussy, her soft moans began once more. As his fingers slipped across her pussy lips she gasped loudly.

The young man took his hands off her pussy for a moment, but she immediately said, "No, don't stop, please". He didn't need an excuse to continue and soon she was moaning like she does as an orgasm begins to build deep within.

He slowly pushed two fingers deep into her wet pussy and moved them in and out vigorously. With his other hand he began softly stroking her clitoris. I now managed to drag myself away from watching and took an engorged nipple in my mouth and sucked hard. My wife was writhing on the bed just about ready to come.

As I finished sucking the other nipple I slid my hand down to her pussy as a message to our friend to stop.

My wife let out a deep "no" as his hands pulled away.

* * *

"We'll let you come very soon," I said, "but I think you should know that our guest has a huge bulge in his trousers caused by you, so I think it's only fair that you help him out a little. What do you think?"

"You mean…?" she said.

"I looked at the young man and said, would you like her to help you with that bulge?" "Oh, god yes" he replied in an instant.

"So, it's settled then".

"Why don't you take off you clothes?" I said to the waiter, "Ready to take your pleasure".

As I was talking, I casually brushed my fingers across her pussy lips.

As the young man began to strip, I relayed details about her new lover to my wife lying prone, blindfold and naked on the bed. I described how our guest had an impressive erection, that his cock was circumcised, rather thick with a luscious bulbous end and that she was definitely going to enjoy him. He looked huge, but he was probably about average. The heat of the moment made his dick look massive.

When he was naked I suggested to our guest that he go and suck her nipples again while I got undressed.

My darling's moans once more began in earnest as her nipples were sucked into an eager mouth. As he slurped over her very puffy nipples and squeezed her tits, I knelt down by her head and kissed her passionately. Her tongue eagerly sought out mine and I could feel her urgency.

All this time our guest was still sucking her engorged nipples and she was letting out soft moans I was removing my clothes.

When I was naked with my dick harder than I had ever felt it, I asked our guest if he would like to taste her pussy. He didn't answer, just dived between her legs and started licking her copious juices.

My wife's moans were now very loud.

"Oh, god," she moaned in ecstasy. "let me come soon…".

"Guest first," I said.

The waiter stood at the foot of the bed. His mouth and face were covered in my wife's pussy juices. His dick was rigidly pointing upwards and he was looking at the naked woman on the bed with greedy eyes.

"May I…? he looked at me imploringly.

"One moment," I said moving to untie her wrists.

When she was loose, I took off her blindfold so she could see our young friend.

"Is that what you want," I asked, pointing to the waiter's engorged dick.

"Oh, God, yeeees, please…… now…." she almost screamed and lunged forward on the bed.

The lust in her eyes was intense. I had never seen her so aroused and she was focused on one thing.

To my surprise instead of pulling the waiter towards her onto the bed, she pushed him backwards and knelt down in front of him on the floor. She grabbed his thick cock with her right hand and took the bulbous, cut cock into her mouth. The waiter moaned as Anne's soft lips encircled the glans.

Anne was in a frenzy, she was now cupping his balls with one hand and grabbing and squeezing his butt cheek with the other, all the while moving up and down his thick cock with her mouth. She was looking intently up at him as she mouth-fucked him.

I hadn't moved an inch. I was entranced by the sight of my wife's lips encircling another man's cock and her fingers caressing and fondling his balls.

The waiter's eyes were locked onto my wife's. He was grunting and moaning at each thrust into her willing mouth. His thrusts were becoming more forceful and soon Anne was taking a huge length of thick cock, it must have been penetrating deep into her throat.

Normally with me she kept her fingers firmly on my cock so I couldn't go too deeply into her mouth. Not today though. She was letting her young lover totally fuck her mouth. She made some gagging noises, but didn't let up.

As the waiter's grunts became more intense and more rapid. And as he began to thrust more forcefully into her mouth, I expected her to grab his cock with her hand and finish him off. But what she did was put both hands on his butt cheeks and drive his cock faster and faster over her soft lips and into her hungry mouth.

Then it happened. I could see the young man's balls tighten. As they did he let out an almighty grunt and deep scream from his throat and thrust his cock madly in and out of my wife's waiting mouth.

The waiter closed his eyes as the first spurts hit the back of Anne's throat, but my wife's eyes were glued to the pained expression on his face. She was letting him fuck her mouth and drinking in the thick white cum.

I could see the spunk pulsing along his dick before it shot forcefully into my wife's more than willing fuck hole. White streams of spunk were seeping out the corners of her mouth and down her chin. She was still pulling him back and forth with both hands.

As the frenzied pumping slowed down and the young man's grunts calmed, Anne pulled her mouth lovingly off the spent dick and licked the last white globules dripping from the end.

The young man hadn't yet kissed her and while I stood wondering if he would, transfixed by spunk dribbling down my wife's beaming face, she stood up and placed her lips on my mouth. I felt her tongue go deep in my mouth thrusting a thick load of spunk onto my tongue. I swallowed it greedily and groans of satisfaction start to well in her throat.

I was still feeling surges of jealousy that she had done to a stranger what she had never, ever done to me, but the eroticism of the moment pushed such feelings to one side.

As we kissed passionately, we fell back on the bed. My throbbing dick reached her engorged pussy lips and I pushed it hungrily into my wife's slippery hole. We both let out a moan as my dick plunged in to her dripping wet pussy.

I began to slam my dick faster and faster into her and grabbed hold of her tits and nipples roughly as I pounded her. She was moaning and calling out, urging me to come.

I pulled her legs up to her waist and slowed down my thrusts, easing my dick slowly out, then slamming it back in. With each thrust she screamed in pleasure. When my dick reached her outer pussy lips, I could feel her release of breath and her exquisite agony as she had to wait for the next thrust.

But I couldn't hold on, my thrusts were speeding up again, she was squealing in pleasure. I was grunting with each thrust. Soon my grunts became faster and faster as I released a stream of hot cum into my wife. As I did so, she orgasmed and thrashed about on the bed as I continued to pound her pussy.

My spurting thrusts seem to go on for ever, and I was imagining how much cum I was leaving in her pussy. As my movements slowed down, I licked the rest of the waiter's cum from her lips and chin, whispered thank you and slowly pulled out of her well-used pussy.

Our waiter must have picked up his clothes and slipped out of the room in a rush, because neither of us seemed to notice him leave.

I was in awe at the sight of my wife's soft lips and mouth that had just received a full load of warm spunk from a stranger.

Anne was breathing heavily and sweating in the after glow of orgasm. I kissed her forcefully on the lips again and told her how sexy she looked. But, to my surprise she whispered in my ear that I still had a job to do.

I moved down between her legs and looked at her pussy lips. They were puffy and dark red. Beautifully engorged. As she lay there with her legs wide open I could see globules of my sperm dribbling from her pussy lips.

"Well?" she said, "I'm waiting".

※ ※ ※

I had often talked about doing this to her, but it never felt right after cumming. This time, however, I took one last look and dived between her legs. My tongue caressed her labia softly. She had a very musky smell that made my dick throb. My tongue lapped up the first drops of my sperm mixed in with her juices. I was in ecstasy. I swallowed down all the cum dribbling from her pussy as she pulled my mouth tighter onto her pussy lips.

I could feel another orgasm starting in her body. She pushed me away suddenly and told me to lie on the bed. As I did, she swung herself on top of me and lowered her pussy onto my waiting tongue and mouth.

As her pussy came nearer to my face I could see huge globules of cum ready to drop into my open mouth. My tongue pushed into her pussy and I felt her pussy muscles bear down to expel my cum. To my surprise it gushed over my waiting lips. Copious amounts of pussy juices and cum filled me. I swallowed it all, even enjoying the taste. I sucked and licked and swallowed until suddenly my wife let out a huge scream in orgasm as my tongue finished cleaning out her pussy.

PART THREE
Submitting to a Stranger

3-1. Anne's diary - Preparation

The previous evening we'd both fallen asleep almost immediately, but woke up about three in the morning and talked again about the events over the last few days.

I have to admit, I was still rather surprised by my behavior. I had always known about Matt's erotic desires to see me flaunt myself and show off my body, but I had never felt such urges to go along with this more than a little. I was also stunned to see the effect that a flash of my naked body had on men in general. I'd always been on the conservative side in my choice of clothes and since being with Matt, I naturally hadn't sought the attention of men.

My flagrant exhibitionism was like a drug. I was high on the leering look in men's eyes as they caught a glimpse of my nipple or pussy. Yesterday I had reveled in my ability to make a couple of young men cum at the sight of my naked body. And last night, not only did I fulfill one of Matt's fantasies by letting a stranger touch my body, but I went further than I'd even gone with Matt, by letting the young man dump his load in my mouth. I was enjoying my newly discovered power and I knew I was willing to experience even more - not just to please my husband and carry out his erotic desires, but for me and my own sexual and erotic pleasure.

At the back of my head I was fearful that Matt might suffer jealousy seeing me suck another man's cock, but he seemed fine and was full of praise for all I had done for him.

We slept late after our exertions of the night before and missed breakfast in the hotel. After a snack in a café in Arles, we didn't get home to the villa in Aix until after two. A letter addressed to Matt was waiting in the letterbox. It had been delivered by hand and was handwritten on exquisite parchment. Both of us immediately guessed it was from the exclusive club our neighbor Antoine had mentioned..

The letter, to our surprise, was in English.

> *"This evening at 7 p.m. the Supreme Master will attend at your residence.*
>
> *The presence of yourself and the supplicant at said time indicates that you wish to proceed with the induction process into The Club.*
>
> *You will prepare for the induction with care.*
>
> 1. *The supplicant will obey all instructions from the Supreme Master without question.*
> 2. *The supplicant will wear a shelf bra, a micro thong, a one piece dress of husband's choosing and high heels of at least 4 cm.*
> 3. *The supplicant will have no body hair.*
> 4. *Supplicant's make up will be minimal.*
>
> *The honor of membership in The Club is bestowed only on the most worthy.*
>
> *Be worthy!"*

"Rather pompous," I had said to Matt after reading it through, "They certainly think highly of themselves, let's see whether they are worthy of us."

Matt didn't say much for the next half hour or so. We sat on the veranda and had a bite of lunch.

"So," he finally said, "are you willing to do this?"

"I am if you are," I had replied. I wanted to show these pompous pricks that we were good enough, if not too good, for their club.

"I'll go get the clothes you need, you can prepare your body. Ok?"

"Ok," I said, "But, Matt, are you really ready to go through with this? Do you really want to join this mysterious club? They could ask us to do anything, anything at all. I'll stop whenever you want. All you have to do is tell me. I love you and will do anything to make you happy, but I don't want you to go through any pain or suffering."

Matt didn't answer. "We've only got a few hours," he said and dashed off into Aix. I took that to mean "yes."

3-2. Anne's Diary - Submission

I was now left alone in the villa to prepare my body. First I had to remove my pussy hair for the first time. The thought was actually making me wet.

At five to seven I was standing in our ensuite looking at myself in the mirror. The doorbell rang promptly at seven, but apart from the door opening, I hadn't heard anything, not even any voices.

My reflection was no longer the young woman I'd been twenty years ago, but I wasn't bad for my age, I thought. As requested, or rather demanded, in the letter, I was wearing a new shelf bra that held up my breasts, but teasingly showed my nipples and areolae, Matt had bought me a new micro thong to match the bra. It was so micro that it barely covered by pussy lips. My new heels were dazzlingly high, but certainly showed off my assets. Matt had also decided to buy me a new sundress. It had spaghetti straps, a fitted bustier with four buttons down the front and a full skirt that came to about 10 inches above my knees. Because it was ivory white in color, I could make out my dark ruby nipples through the material and as I cupped my breasts with both hands, I felt my nipples harden. My breasts aren't huge, a decent C-cup, but I had lusciously large areolae and nipples that were quick to harden at the slightest hint of arousal.

The dress really only came down to just below the top of my legs. I lifted the dress slightly and in the reflection I could see the outline of my newly shaved pussy through the material. I had never shaved my pubes before and was quite taken with the novelty. My legs and armpits were also as smooth as I could get using a razor.

Looking at myself, even though I was quite pleased with my look, I was inclined to call the whole thing off. I had my phone in my bag, I could just call Matt and ask him to show the guest out.

What was I thinking, a 38 year old woman dressed like this in front of a stranger.

The wine I had drunk earlier was wearing off, it seemed, so I filled up my glass from the bottle I'd brought into the bathroom and downed a good half glass in one gulp.

I had to admit, though, that the thought of my husband showing me off to the Supreme Master did make my pussy tingle. The fact that he wanted to, was exciting in itself. The fact that someone had demanded to see me dressed like this, sent shivers through my body into the very tips of my nipples and down between my legs. The throbbing in my pussy and my hard nipples poking through my dress were revealing how I really felt.

I hadn't really thought about what this induction would entail. Showing me off to a stranger was one thing, but at the back of my mind I knew what could happen, if I let it. But did I want things to go so far, that was the question. We had decided on our secret word, just in case.

I drank down the rest of my glass and looked once more into the mirror. I knew my husband thought I was sexy. Events over the last few days had made me realise that other men also found me attractive. I realised that we had been fulfilling some of Matt's oldest fantasies since we'd come to France. My husband had dreamed about them for years. Oh god, I thought, I'm getting really wet at the thought of this exhibitionism. For that's what it was, pure exhibitionism.

I took a swig from the wine bottle. had one last glance at myself in the mirror and stepped out into the bedroom.

Matt was sitting in the armchair facing our ensuite and saw me first. Opposite him was the man I presumed was the Supreme

Master who was facing the window, looking away from the bathroom. He didn't turn as I stepped into the room, but continued to sip from his glass. Matt smiled and walked towards me holding out his hand.

"My god you look stunning", he said, "come and meet Master Pascal, the Supreme Master".

He led me by the hand and stood me in front of his chair, a couple of steps away from the surprisingly young man sitting on the bedroom sofa. He was probably mid twenties, well-built, but not too much, with wavy hair and a pleasant face. His face betrayed nothing as he looked appraisingly at me. Matt stood by my side holding my hand.

"Turn round," he said in English, "Let me see you from behind".

I was inclined to tell him what he could do with his command, but the way he said it made my pussy tingle again, and I turned as requested.

"Good, now turn back round and step closer to me."

I turned round and took a step closer.

"Put your hands behind you head and spread your legs," he commanded.

The tone of his voice left no doubt that I would obey.

Tentatively I put my hands behind my head and spread my legs, aware that this stranger could see the outline of my nipples clearly through the ivory colored material and fearful that the wetness in my pussy would betray me. My thong was probably quite wet by now.

❈ ❈ ❈

Master Pascal put his glass down and stood up. He walked up to me, caught my gaze and then looked me up and down taking his time to look at the swell of my breasts and my legs. He then walked slowly round me and back to his seat on the sofa.

"Have you ever undressed your wife for a stranger?" he asked Matt.

"Not really, no," Matt replied, probably wondering whether yesterday's fun counted as such.

"Have you ever watched your wife sucking another man's cock?" he then asked.

"Er, yes", stammered Matt. Master Pascal didn't react.

"And have you ever seen another man's cock slip into your wife's cunt?"

I flinched at the word, but Matt calmly replied, "No, never."

"Is this what you want to happen? Do you want to strip your wife naked for a stranger? Do you want to watch that stranger fuck your wife's mouth? Do you really want to watch that stranger take your wife in front of you? Tell me, is that what you really want?"

Matt hesitated and looked at me, but I was staring at Master Pascal, knowing without a doubt what Matt would say and feeling a surge of lust through my body.

"Yes, that's what I want." He finally said.

I made no outward reaction, but my thong got much wetter. The use of the word cunt about my own pussy, had made me feel so sexy. This was already going way beyond what I had ever imagined. He hadn't even mentioned the club yet, I presumed this was just part of the softening up process.

"What about you supplicant?", he said to me, "Do you want a stranger's cock in your mouth, in your cunt, fucking you to orgasm? Because I'm leaving now unless you can truthfully say you do."

"Yes, I do want it", I said rather too quickly and much to my surprise. And realised that I really did want it, not only to please Matt, but for me. I felt empowered at the thought of this young man wanting me so carnally.

"Will you give me your body for the next few hours to let me do as I wish?"

"I will", was all I said.

"If you please me and I approve, will you give your body to The Club to let its members' do as they wish?"

I looked at Matt wanting reassurance, but he seemed to be in a daze.

"I will", I finally said, wondering what the hell I was letting myself in for.

"Good", said Master Pascal, "we can proceed."

"Matt, remove the supplicant's dress now."

Matt moved behind me, touched my arms and moved them to my sides. From behind he then undid the four buttons slowly and pulled the straps down my arms. I realised he was doing this from behind so that Master Pascal would get the full effect as he stripped me.

✾ ✾ ✾

As the dress fell to the floor, my nipples hardened even more as the material slipped over them.

I put my arms back behind my head and spread my legs again almost unconsciously obeying Master Pascal's silent command.

Master Pascal's face betrayed nothing. His piercing eyes took in my areolae and rock hard nipples being served up by the shelf bra. I was also aware that my pussy lips would be fully visible through the semi-transparent mini-thong.

"Pull off the thong so I can see how wet the supplicant's cunt is," he finally barked to Matt.

Matt, still behind me pulled at the flimsy strap of the thong. The thong came off in one pull.

Now, I felt very vulnerable. I could sense how engorged my pussy lips were and my clit was throbbing.

"Give it to me", the Master said to Matt.

Matt handed my thong to the stranger. Master Pascal brought them to his nose and smiled for the first time since I had come into the room.

"Very nice, very wet, you're almost ready for me."

He slipped my thong into his trouser pocket.

Master Pascal looked at Matt, "take off all your clothes and come and sit next to me on the sofa for a better view."

While Matt began taking off his clothes the Master came and

stood in front of me and ran his hands over my body. He cupped my breasts, as if feeling the weight, and rubbed his thumbs twice over my hard nipples. I gasped as he did so and felt my juices running down my leg.

The Master's hands continued to knead my breasts and tease my nipples. I was in ecstasy. I hardly noticed Matt move to the sofa and sit there in the nude with a raging hard on, revealing how he felt about the proceedings so far.

Master Pascal moved his hands slowly down my tummy and his left hand continued over my bald mound to my sopping cunt. His middle finger slipped easily inside me. As he pulled it out there was a juicy plop. He brought his finger up to my mouth and without a word spoken I sucked the juices off his finger.

"Good girl", he said. "This is going to work, very well".

"Matt, take off her bra and let me see her totally nude."

Matt got up and I noticed how huge his erection really was. It pleased me immensely. Matt undid my bra and removed it. I was now totally naked in front of a stranger while my husband looked on.

"Very nice, Matt. You have a very sexy wife. We are going to enjoy fucking her".

I felt myself blush at his words and wondered whom he meant by "we", but was past caring. I felt as if I could cum right now.

As if sensing my feelings, the Master then turned to me and said, "Turn round now and touch your toes, but make sure you keep your legs spread."

I hesitated a second, realising that such a stance would really show me truly naked with nothing left to the imagination.

"Are you defying me?" the Master asked.

I turned and bent to touch my toes with my legs apart. I envisaged what I would look like to the two men behind me. I doubted my husband had ever seen me so utterly exposed before. I felt brazen and very sexy being ogled so openly.

Master Pascal came up behind me and without warning stuck two fingers in my cunt. I gasped in surprise and pleasure.

I was sopping wet and moaned as the Master moved his fingers in and out. Once his fingers were covered in my juices, he moved one finger to my asshole. I gasped out in loud pain as his finger slipped in almost unopposed and began to move in and out rapidly.

Just as I began to feel my first orgasm approaching he took out his fingers.

"Now supplicant, you will undress me".

I stood in front of him and began to unbutton his shirt. I then slipped it off his shoulders and arms. I bent down to undo his shoes and slipped them off with his socks. "Can't have him in socks and boxers", I laughed to myself.

Then I unclasped his trousers and pulled them down. He lifted each foot in turn to help me. The Master was now standing in his boxers. It was more than obvious that he was ready for action.

I knelt in front of him making sure I was side on to the sofa. "I want Matt to have the best view as I suck the Master's cock," brazenly ran through my mind as I did it. I realized this was the point of absolute no return. I looked at Matt as I knelt down and he smiled lovingly at me. His cock still told me all I needed to know.

I was eye height with the Master's cock as I pulled his boxers over the bulge. I didn't immediately look at it, but concentrated on getting the boxers completely off. But once that was done I returned to my kneeling position and had my first close-up view of the Master's thick, veiny dick.

The Master wasn't huge, but he seemed bigger than Matt, at least in terms of girth. He was totally shaved, making him seem bigger, I thought. I had never seen a man fully shaved. "It looks good", flashed through my mind.

"Well?" the Master said.

I knew what he meant. I looked quickly at Matt who was pumping his own dick, and then licked the pre-cum off the end of the Master's cock. He moaned as I did it and then moaned even louder as I wrapped my lips around the end of his cock and began to move up and down.

I used all my blow job skills on Master Pascal. I licked him up and down the shaft, took his balls in my mouth, teased the ribbed part at the end and took him as far into my mouth as I could. The sounds the Master was making encouraged my to keep on going.

"Matt, come and kneel next to your wife", the Master suddenly said. Matt didn't hesitate and knelt next to his naked wife in front of Pascal. His hard on was begging for relief, but I knew he would want to keep it for as long as possible.

"Kiss her on the mouth", the Master said.

Matt eagerly began to kiss me on the lips. I tasted of another man's pre-cum and it excited him even more as he locked tongues with me in a frenzied passionate kiss.

Master Pascal stopped our passion by placing his dick between us and guiding it into my mouth again.

"No hands, now", he commanded, and began moving in and out of my mouth inches from Matt's face. His movements became faster and faster. He was truly fucking my mouth. Matt was probably wondering how I was managing not to gag as the Master plunged it ever deeper past my lips.

The Master's hand was on the back of my head now, pulling me closer to him. I was making gagging noises as the rigid cock moved towards the back of my throat, but he continued regardless, fucking my mouth mercilessly.

Suddenly I gagged quite strongly and began to cough. The Master pulled out his cock and spoke angrily to me, "Relax, you can take it, I'm going to come in your mouth and then you are going to kiss your husband and let him enjoy my cum too. Any more disobedience and I will have to punish you. Understood?"

I had never let Matt cum in my mouth and now for the second time in two days a stranger was going to deposit his cum in my throat. Despite my urge to gag I was determined to prove myself to this arrogant man and nodded my understanding. Once again I opened my mouth wide. The Master shoved his dick in my mouth roughly and began fucking my mouth even more vigorously. Within 5 or 6 thrusts it was obvious he was beginning to cum. His hand held my head firmly and pulled my mouth over his cock.

The Master began to grunt loudly and I felt the first spurts of cum, small spurts at first, then suddenly my mouth was full of the salty liquid. Pride wouldn't let me gag. I swallowed some of the hot cum, but used the rest to glide my lips and tongue across the engorged cock.

The Master's rhythm slowed and he pulled his spent dick out of my mouth. Cum was running down my chin and onto my breast as I pulled Matt to my and kissed him passionately. I was proud of myself and wanted to show Matt how much cum I had taken for him. Matt devoured my spunky kiss and even licked the globs off my chin and breast.

I looked at Matt after our kiss. He had Master Pascal's spunk on his lips and there was a large dollop of pre-cum trailing from his cock.

I had never felt so turned on and was now desperate to come. I hoped the Master would let me soon.

The Master grabbed me roughly by the hand and pulled me to the bed.

"On your back with your knees bent", he said to me. "Matt, come over here so you can watch closely as I penetrate your wife's cunt".

Matt walked to the bed and stood next to the Master.

He and Matt were now at the foot of the bed. I was on my back on the bed. My knees were up and together. I was relieved that neither man could yet see how wet my pussy was.

"Matt," said the Master, "I am now going to fuck your wife's cunt" - I squirmed in anticipation as he said it - "and I am going to deposit my cum deep inside my. I expect you to clean me off afterwards and prepare me to take her again. Understood?.

"Yes", said Matt, his cock twitching with desire.

❀ ❀ ❀

"Your wife is now going to slowly spread her legs and reveal her sopping wet fuck-hole to me. You will then guide my prick into her cunt and watch as her cunt lips swallow my dick."

Matt was looking at the Master's rock hard prick and I knew he had to do as he said. After all our fantasy talk, I knew how much he longed to see that dick enter my cunt.

Matt was watching in awe as I slowly parted my legs revealing my engorged cunt lips. I'm sure he could see my juices running down my crack. (Afterwards he told me that he had never seen me looking sexier than at this moment and longed to come in me right then).

When my legs were as wide as they could go the Master climbed on to the bed and positioned himself to enter me. His cock was at the ready and I realised I wanted it inside me now.

I suddenly realised that the Master hadn't even kissed me yet. As the thought flashed through my mind he suddenly bent over me and shoved his tongue deep in my mouth. Our lips were locked as I kissed him feverishly. The Master's left hand was roughly squeezing my breast and his dick was rubbing my pussy lips.

"Matt, guide me in", the Master said as he pulled free of our kiss.

Much to my surprise Matt didn't hesitate, he moved up to the Master's side and lightly took hold of his cock and placed it in position at the entrance to my sopping wet cunt. I saw his hand shaking, he was so excited.

The Master wasted no time thrusting slowly into me. Matt was watching in a trance as, for the first time, he saw another man penetrate me. I gasped and threw back my head as the Master's cock reached its full length and then began to slowly retreat from my cunt.

After several slow strokes he began to speed up. I was gasping and screaming as he slammed into my cunt. My hands grasped hold of the Master's ass and pulled him back and forth into me.

After a few minutes I screamed out loudly as my first orgasm hit me. My body shook as he continued to pummel my cunt. He slowed down his thrusts and in a frenzy I grabbed his face and kissed him deeply begging him to speed up.

The Master continued to tease and suddenly pulled his cock out of my cunt. I was now in a total frenzy begging him to fuck me. I don't think Matt had ever heard such language from his normally demure wife.

The Master now turned me onto my stomach and pulled my ass into the air, spread my legs and thrust into me doggy style.

I screamed in orgasmic ecstasy again. I began panting heavily and grunted with every inward thrust. In this position his cock felt absolutely huge and I couldn't get enough. I just wanted the Master to fill me.

Once more the Master slowed down his thrusting and with his fingers rubbed my cunt juices over my asshole. Then, without warning, he thrust a finger quite roughly into my virgin ass. I whimpered in pain and lust and began panting even more, before exploding with another massive orgasm. He didn't let up, his finger thrust ever deeper into my ass.

I was in ecstasy, sweating profusely and grunting wildly again.

The Master stopped thrusting and stayed still with his cock deep in my cunt. I began to buck and thrust back onto him. As I did, he slowly withdrew his rigid cock, no doubt glistening with my juices.

The Master just spread my legs and thrust his cock into my puffy cunt. I gasped in shock. And the heavy panting started again. He was mauling my tits wildly and pulling my nipples as he rode my, slamming his cock against my cunt lips.

My breathing was becoming louder and louder, my pants were becoming loud grunts and suddenly I let out a piercing orgasmic scream as I felt the Master's jism spurt into my gaping cunt. He pumped and pumped until he was dry, then pulled his limp cock from my drained body. I just lay on the bed with my legs sprawled. I could feel the warm spunk dribbling from my cunt.

I looked at the man who had just fucked me as he stood up at the end of the bed. His cock was no longer rigid, but semi-erect, covered in our juices. Matt was standing next to him. Matt's cock was still rock hard and no doubt ready for action. I could see dribbles of pre-cum on the head.

As I looked away from Matt's cock, I remembered the Master's words about cleaning him after he had fucked my cunt.

The Master turned to face my husband.

"Get to work, I need to be clean before I fuck the supplicant's ass."

I'm not sure what Matt was thinking at that moment. When the Master said he was going to fuck my ass, I felt an involuntary spasm in my asshole and couldn't help but put my fingers over my still pulsating clitoris.

Slowly Matt knelt in front of the Master. He glanced at me for a second before the Master took his flaccid cock and pushed it between Matt's lips. As the cock disappeared into my husband's mouth, my fingers slipped into my slippery cunt and I began to move them slowly in and out. Watching my husband lick and suck the Master's cock was unbelievably erotic.

Matt copied what I normally did to him and was looking up into the Master's eyes as he vigorously sucked and licked the Master's cum and my juices from the Master's thick cock.

Matt seemed to be satisfied it was clean and he started to stand up, but the Master pressed his hand onto Matt's head and continued to move his cock in and out of Matt's mouth. Matt didn't take his eyes from the Master's gaze, but appeared surprised at this turn in events. He was probably as shocked and amazed as I was that the Master's cock was once more getting hard. Matt's eyes were still fixed on the Master's as the cock was once more full size.

The Master was definitely fully erect again and began thrusting into Matt's mouth with force. His hand held Matt in place and Matt had guessed what would happen soon. I just hoped he knew how to relax his throat muscles to stop himself gagging. Matt's eye's looked to the side for a moment and no doubt saw me watching him have his mouth fucked. Matt's cock oozing pre-cum as he saw me watching him taking a big cock in the mouth.

Matt had no time for finesse. This was the Master fucking his mouth, no more, no less. The Master's breathing was gaining pace and he was starting to make the little grunting noises that preceded his orgasms. Matt seemed to brace himself. He jolted as a little spurt of cum hit the back of his throat. Suddenly the Master let out another grunt and a second, much bigger spurt of hot cum filled Matt's mouth, followed by another smaller one and finally another. He swallowed some of the hot cum and some of it dribbled out of his mouth and down his chin. The Master kept pumping until the last drops had spilled from his cock.

"Swallow it", the Master commanded, "and then lick me clean".

Matt did as he was told and swallowed everything he had in his mouth.

As he swallowed I came to him and began to lick the drops off his chin and kissed him passionately. "that was so hot," I said.

"Ok, Matt, now it's your turn," the Master said. "I want to watch you fill your wife's cunt with spunk. You cock looks like it's ready to blow."

"Lie on the bed and she will ride you".

Matt lay back on the bed his dick ramrod stiff in anticipation. I climbed on top of him and took a deep breath as his cock slipped slickly into my stretched, velvety cunt. I knew he wouldn't last very long even in my gaping cunt. I felt so smooth, wet and big. The Master knelt between Matt's legs and pawed my breasts and nipples as I rode my husband. He pulled back my head and stuck his tongue down my throat as I moaned in lust.

I was too far gone to notice much but I did feel Matt start to make his orgasm noises, then felt the cum surging up his dick. Matt kept cumming and cummin. I'd never felt him shoot so much cum in his life, probably because he was watching his wife locking lips with this strange man while she fondled his erection.

As I lifted myself off his spent cock, my cunt lips plopped and spunk began running down my leg.

"Go sit on Matt's mouth and let him clean you out. If he does a good job, I'll let him clean you out again when I come again. If you come before he's finished and I find any spunk left on your cunt lips, ass or legs Matt will be taking it in the ass."

❀ ❀ ❀

I moved up to place my swollen pussy over Matt's face. His tongue began lapping up his spunk mixed in with my cunt juices. As he slurped and swallowed I began squirming and panting, ready for another orgasm. Matt tried desperately not to lick my clit and his tongue searched my asshole and the tops of my legs for any last globs of his spunk. Matt's face was covered in our juices, but he was past caring. Suddenly my orgasm sent a shudder through my body. I fell back off Matt and onto the bed. I was shattered.

"On your knees, supplicant, I'm going to inspect you."

Matt sat on the edge of the bed with spunk and juices still plastered across his face. I rolled on to my front and raised my ass in the air with my legs spread. I could feel the Master roughly pawing my thighs and cunt lips. He then told me to grab both of my ass cheeks and show him my asshole.

I did as he commanded.

"Good job, Matt, she's clean."

I went to let go of my cheeks.

"Not yet, supplicant. Keep your hole wide open."

I tensed, sensing what the Master intended to do.

"Make me hard, Matt."

Once again Matt began to lick and suck the Master's cock while I lay prostrate on the bed with my asshole wide open.

In seconds the Master's dick began to grow. He was insatiable.

❀ ❀ ❀

The Master now told Matt to guide his cock into my ass. I felt Matt's hesitation for a second, but the Master just said, "Yes, Matt, I am going to come in her ass and you're going to help, do it!"

Matt knew I was an ass virgin and worried that I might not want to lose it to a stranger. He was probably also a little jealous, as he wasn't the one to take me first in the ass.

"Please, Master Pascal," I said as subserviently as possible, could you please use a little oil"

"Get some oil," he barked at Matt, who disappeared into the bathroom for a second.

Matt came back with some oil and poured it over my asshole.

"On my cock too," the Master said.

When the Master's cock was well lubed, Matt took hold of the thick cock and placed it by my puckered asshole. The Master slowly pushed. I squealed at first with the pain, but tried to relax my ass muscles. As I got used to the feeling of being stuffed in the ass, I soon began to pant heavily again as my ass swallowed the Master bit by bit until it felt like most of his cock was buried deep inside my rear.

I had my third massive orgasm and began to pant heavily again.

The Master must have noticed Matt's cock was hard again, because he pushed me towards the edge of the bed and told Matt to fill my mouth. Matt moved in front of me and I saw how hard he was once more. I smiled up at him and willingly took him deep in my mouth. I tried to keep my eyes on his, but the Master's thrusts were becoming frantic and I couldn't concentrate. Matt was also pumping his dick into my mouth in a frenzy. It occurred to me that I had never allowed him to shoot his load into my mouth.

The Master had now begun to grunt forcefully. His cock thrusts became more urgent and just as I screamed with another orgasm he made his deepest thrust yet and filled my virgin ass with his creamy spunk. The Master thrust and thrust and grunted in pleasure as he filled me up.

My screams were muffled by my husband's rough thrusting in my mouth - the polite Matt had gone, replaced by a man intent on his own pleasure. As the Master pumped his load into my ass, Matt deposited a massive load of cum in my throat. I felt the spurts hit the back of my throat and I swallowed as quickly as I could to stop myself gagging.

Both men pulled their wasted cocks from my body and I flopped exhausted onto the bed. Spunk was dripping from my now deflowered hole, my lips still had dollops of Matt's spunk stuck to them.

Matt kissed me and we fell onto the bed next to each other. Locked together we fell into a post orgasmic sleep in seconds.

We didn't even notice when Master Pascal left.

We woke up the next morning with the sun streaming through the window. We kissed lovingly and as Matt's cock grew we began to make long slow love. "I love you," said Matt, "you are the sexiest woman alive. Thank you for fulfilling so many of my fantasies."

"I love you too", I said. "Thank you for letting me experience such pleasure. Do you think we got into *The Club*?"

PART FOUR

Supplicant Wife

4-1. Outing Anne

Anne's Diary - Saturday

I woke up this morning feeling free and liberated. I couldn't believe how far I had come in less than a week. I couldn't believe that my loving husband was encouraging me to pursue such sexual and erotic pleasures. As Matt had explained, we are in a foreign country, far from home, the sun is shining and we are free to enjoy life to the full and take all the opportunities we are offered.

Matt had talked about "liberating my inner slut". I had always been offended by the word "slut", but last night I had certainly liberated something inside me and reached some erotic peaks I had never before experienced. My pussy and ass felt as if they were still quivering from the poundings I had enjoyed and no doubt my breath reeked of stale spunk.

After a relaxing shower, I put on a short flowery summer dress with a micro thong and my favorite Freya plunge bra that gives me a superb cleavage (or so Matt is always telling me).

Matt was still asleep when I had finished dressing, so I decided to pop out for some fresh bread and croissants.

I grabbed my phone and purse, put on my comfortable leopard skin heels and skipped out the front door turning up the hill towards the *boulangerie*. One of the best things about France for me is the *boulangerie* and the hot, fresh bread available each morning.

I had only walked a few yards, when someone called out my name. I turned to see Antoine, our neighbor, leaning out the window of a sporty little car. Not exactly what I'd expected him to drive.

"Anne," he said, "So glad I caught you, you're looking ravishing again, this morning, I have some good news for you."

"Good morning," I said, blushing slightly at his compliment, but enjoying it immensely.

"The Supreme Master was pleased with you last night. You have passed the first test and will attend our next meeting."

"First test? There's more than one?" I answered somewhat contemptuously thinking all the while what more I could do to prove myself.

"Oh, yes. You can't expect to be made a member of such an exclusive club after just one short test. Now, jump in and I'll take you for a spin."

"No need, Antoine, I'm only dashing to the *boulangerie* for a baguette and croissants."

"Oh, but I insist. I have some ideas to help you with the final step."

Antoine jumped out and ran round to open the door for me. "Quite sprightly for an old man," I thought.

I slid into the car as elegantly as I could, flashing only a modicum of thigh in the process. To my pleasure I noticed that Antoine took in a fair helping of my cleavage as he shut the door.

Antoine shot off up the road. Within a couple of minutes we had passed the *boulangerie* and Aix was in his rear-view mirror.

When I looked at him quizzically, he smiled and said, "I'd like to show you something, my dear Anne, I'll drop you back home soon."

"I'll have to call Matt," I said, "he'll be worried, if he wakes up and I'm not there."

Antoine pulled the car over and took my phone out of my hand.

"I'll send him a text to make him happy."

Antoine tapped away for a few minutes, then passed me the phone, before hurtling off up the road again. I took a look at the message he had sent to my husband: "Matt, your ravishing wife is spending the day with me. Reply to this message with 'I accept' and I'll keep you updated as our adventure unfolds. Any other calls or messages and it's radio silence."

Antoine's English was flawless, but I was insulted that he had presumed I'd go along with him for the day without asking and was taunting Matt like this.

"I never said I'd spend the day with you," I snapped, "and why would Matt go along with your ridiculous idea?"

"Ah, but you want to come along, I know. Just as I know your husband will relish our adventures today. He will crave every message I send him"

Antoine continued as the phone beeped incoming message, "Just as I know you will show me your delicious tits in half an hour or so."

I turned in my seat to look at him, "That's preposterous, why would I want to do that?"

"Because I will ask you to," he said looking me in the eye.

"I know you are ready to submit to me as you submitted to the Master yesterday."

My cunt quivered again and I knew he was right despite my protestations.

I checked the message with a little trepidation, I wasn't sure what I wanted or expected Matt to do: "I accept."

As I read it I could feel the wetness between my legs.

"He accepted, didn't he," Antoine said with a laugh. "I knew he would. He wants the thrill of hearing about what I'm doing to you today. He's probably lying in bed now with his hands fondling his own rock hard erection just in anticipation."

What could I say, I knew Antoine was probably right. So, I settled back to enjoy the ride next to this persuasive French gentleman who had a way of making me comfortable even when I was feeling the deepest discomfort.

Fifteen minutes later we passed through Les Mattes, a small village near the foot of Mont Ste Victoire. A mile or so further on and Antoine stopped the car close to a footpath leading up the mountain. Antoine jumped out and came to assist me out of the car, no doubt once again enjoying the view of my breasts and thighs.

The mountain peak looked majestic in the distance and the scent of thyme was quite overpowering. Antoine took a picnic basket, that I hadn't noticed, from the back seat and moved towards the trail leading upwards.

"Before we go, we'll text a message. I think it's time to let your darling Matt know what's happening."

I went to hand him the phone, but he refused it and said, "No, you write it, your fingers a more adept than mine. Write what I say: 'Beautiful day. Going for a stroll in the hills. My cunt is already wet and willing. Longing for him to tell me to remove my bra. xxx.'"

I wrote what he said and felt my cunt muscles spasm as I pressed send.

"Leave your bra in the car," Antoine commanded.

I looked him defiantly in the eye while I removed it from under my dress. The dress had minimal support for my breasts, so after I had dropped my bra onto the front seat, I tied the strap around my neck tighter, to keep them in check. I knew they would bounce as I walked in my heels, but knew that was the effect men, for some reason, loved.

"Excellent, let's go." And with that Antoine set off along the trail.

Walking on a stony, dusty trail through the pine trees in three inch heels is not the easiest thing to do, but I stumbled onward as best I could. The peak of the mountain is over 3,000 feet high and even a seasoned rambler would need a good four hours to reach it, so I wasn't intending going too far up the slopes.

Antoine kept looking back at me and smiling, whether at my clumsy stumbling or the charms of my body, I couldn't say. After a few hundred yards we came to an opening in the trees. Antoine had already set out a rug when I arrived.

As he set out the bread and cheese I suddenly realized I was famished.

I plonked down on the rug and took a hunk of baguette.

"Not so fast," my lovely, "that piece of bread should be worth at least a glimpse of your tits."

Antoine looked me up and down as if appraising me as he spoke.

"I liked what I saw from my balcony yesterday, but now I want a closer look. Your nipples looked exquisite and I can see you rather like the idea of dropping your top, those hard nipples are an absolute give-away," he laughed.

Antoine was right, my nipples had hardened at his words and my cunt muscles spasmed again.

"Text Matt while you're thinking, say. 'Enjoying picnic in woods. About to take off my top so Antoine can feast on my rigid nipples.' I'm sure he'll appreciate the ambiguity of 'feast'."

I wrote the text as ordered all the time knowing I would do as I was told.

After pressing send, I reached behind my neck and undid the strap. Slowly I pulled down the front of my dress so Antoine had a clear view of my breasts. My nipples were rock hard.

Antoine murmured his approval, "Your tits are even better close up." As he spoke he reached out and brushed my left nipple with his thumb. I moaned with pleasure and felt my cunt getting even wetter.

As he continued to brush my nipple, he said, "Now take a

picture of yourself and send it to your husband, then we can eat something."

I took the picture as Antoine wanted and sent it to Matt. I only hoped Antoine was right and that Matt was enjoying our day out.

For the next quarter of an hour we ate and drank. Antoine had laid on quite a spread, with various cheeses, hams and patés. The rosé was still well chilled and it went well with the meal. Antoine was also a cultivated companion. He talked about Provence and Cézanne. He was an avid fan of the painter and promised to point out all the places Cézanne had frequented in the area during my stay.

I was laughing and giggling at his stories and totally forgot my bare breasts.

When we had finished Antoine packed away the basket and said he wanted to show me another of his and Cézanne's favorite spots a few hundred yards further up the mountain. I stood up and went to fasten my straps back on.

"Oh, no, my lovely. You're now going to take your dress off completely, aren't you?"

"I am? But, what if someone comes?"

"That's highly unlikely at this time of year, but I'm sure anyone that happened to pass would be most appreciative of your charms. So, hand me your dress now and I'll put it in the basket."

I pulled my dress over my head and passed it to him. I felt very vulnerable in just my leopard heels and micro thong. My bare cunt lips were probably visible through the minuscule patch of cloth and my bum cheeks were totally bare.

"Thank you. Now text your husband this: 'Cunt juices flowing even more. Antoine has my dress. Walking along track in thong and heels only. Wish you could see my tits bounce.'"

I did as he said and we continued along the track. Every so often we came out of the forest into an open area. At first I walked even more tentatively, but Antoine said I should be proud of my body.

Progress was still slow because of my footwear, but Antoine refused my request to walk in bare feet. He said that real women wear heels and that I was a real woman. A few days earlier I would have told him that was sexist crap. I knew that when this fantasy period was over, I would go back to thinking that way.

We had been climbing steadily higher for the last half hour and now had a spectacular view back towards Aix and over the countryside down to Marseille. The airport was visible in the distance as well as the factories near the coastal lakes.

"Text your husband again, write this: 'Antoine wants me to take off my thong. If I do I'm sure he'll want to fuck me. You may answer this text with one word, yes or no. Do I take it off now?'"

I couldn't believe I was writing the message. It must have been a mere 15 seconds after I pressed send that the phone beeped incoming message.

"Yes" was all it said.

"Well," said Antoine, "It's obvious he said yes, so give me your thong."

I pulled the thong down to my feet and stepped out of it. I knew it would be rather wet. Antoine took it from my hand, brought it up to his face and breathed in the aroma of my juices.

"Heavenly, you smell divine, my lovely."

Antoine put my thong in his pocket and then placed the picnic basket next to a large flat rock. "Come over here," he said.

I moved over next to the rock. As I did so, he spread the picnic rug over the rock. I had a good idea what he had in mind and was looking forward to enjoying a more seasoned lover. Matt's rapid "yes" message had left me in no doubt that he approved. What more could a woman ask for?

When the rug was ready Antoine stood in front of me and took both my breasts in his hands. He squeezed and fondled them for a moment before tweaking my nipples with his thumbs. My legs almost gave way when he did. Standing next to him like this I could see the extent of his hard on and knew how excited I was making him.

His left hand continued to fondle my tits and nipples while his right hand slipped between my legs. Two fingers slipped inside me and I gasped in pleasure. As he pulled his fingers slowly out of my cunt, he ran them up and over my clit. I shivered in ecstasy.

"On the rock." He ordered, "Lie down on your back."

He helped me up and I took up my position on the rock. It was large enough for me to lie at full stretch.

I put my arms over my head to show off my breasts and spread my legs wide to give Antoine a full view of my sopping wet cunt. At that moment, I totally grasped the meaning the word "slut" in a positive sense. I was enjoying flaunting my body.

Antoine didn't move, he just looked at me. I saw his eyes devour my cunt and then my breasts and back to my cunt. I knew I was the one with the power.

"Touch yourself slowly."

I moved my right hand towards my pussy.

"No, with your left hand. I want to see your wedding ring while you make yourself come for me."

I swapped hands and moved the unfamiliar left hand to my cunt lips and caressed them gently. My eyes closed as I slipped my fingers between my labia and pushed them deeply inside and slowly moved them in and out. For a moment I opened my eyes to look at Antoine. I was shocked to see him filming me with my own phone, but the waves of pleasure building inside, drew me back to my fingers caressing my cunt.

As my cunt muscles began to tremble slightly, my fingers moved from my cunt lips to my clit and circled it gently. With my right hand I was roughly pulling on my breast and nipple. As the first flood of my orgasm hit me I arched my back, flung back my head and screamed in exquisite agony, pulling viciously at my nipple and rubbing my clit in a frenzy.

As the waves of orgasm subsided, my fingers slowed to a gentle caress and my body relaxed back onto the rug. I was quite spent.

Antoine fiddled with the phone for a moment and then looked at me.

"I hope you enjoyed that as much as I did. I'm sure your husband will love your performance."

"What? You've sent it to him?"

"Of course, I didn't want him to miss out. I should think it'll keep him occupied for some time."

As he spoke I heard voices coming up the track. I started to get up, but Antoine told me to stay put.

"It'll be some friends of mine. I told them we'd be here. They all love a beautiful woman. And they particularly like beautiful sluts. And you, my lovely, are one beautiful slut."

I didn't know how to react to that, but before I could say anything two youngish men and a woman came through the trees.

They shouted hello to Antoine and then made appreciative noises about his slut on the rocks. I didn't move, just stared brazenly back at them as they took in my vulnerable body.

"Open your legs wide again, I want them to see your cunt properly," Antoine commanded.

Naturally, I submissively complied.

"You just missed a superb show," Antoine said to the group, "but luckily I have it on her phone. I'll send you copies later."

"Antoine," I said, "I never said you could film me and I certainly don't want copies sent to all and sundry."

"You should be proud that I want to share you. I'm sure your husband will willingly send out the movie of you. We'll let him decide. But, now," he continued, turning to the newcomers, "who wants to try out her cunt first? Or should we let her decide?"

He turned back to look at me. Even though I felt like a lump of meat, my cunt muscles were already quivering in anticipation and I'm sure they could all see how wet I was becoming again.

4-2. Three's Company - *Anne's Diary*

"Well, my beautiful slut. There are four of us here, you have three orifices. You can decide who gets which or do you want us all in one? What's it to be? Or should we let your husband decide? Yes, I like that idea. Text him for me." With that Antoine handed me my phone.

"I think you should say: 'About to have three cocks. Your choice: three different holes or three same. Reply with cunt, mouth, ass or all.'

While I was writing the message the three men were already removing their clothes. Antoine's dick was by far the thickest, but the blonde friend could beat him for length. The girl stayed fully clothed for some reason.

Antoine climbed onto the rock next to me and put his fingers on my cunt lips. Roughly, he pushed a couple of fingers inside. I shuddered. He smirked at my wetness and lifted up his fingers to show the others. She's gagging for us. I'll take her cunt first as she and her husband can't make up their mind. My phone beeped. A message had arrived from Matt. Just one word: 'cunt' meaning my husband wanted them all to take me in my cunt.

"By the end of this," I thought, "I'll have had more men this week than I've had in 20 years. If that's not slutty, I don't know what is. I hope I'm making my husband happy and proud."

Antoine now knelt between my splayed legs with his thick cock pointing straight at me. His balls were huge and dangled down a long way between his legs. I felt like touching them, they looked so inviting, but as I looked from his dick to his face, he moved on top of me. The man I had thought to be a typical French gentleman was now inches from my cunt. I put my arms behind my head as his face reached my tits.

He grabbed the left breast clumsily with his hand and sucked my nipple between his lips. It felt divine and sent shivers straight to my clit. He did the same to my right nipple and I shuddered involuntarily. This made him smile at me as his lips locked onto mine. His tongue forced its way into my mouth and I moaned with pleasure.

I felt totally wanton as his thick cock moved against my cunt lips. Ever so slowly he pushed his way inside. Deeper and deeper and deeper. I felt utterly full. He then retreated slowly and almost pulled out totally before plunging back into me with a grunt. I squealed in delight. His hands roughly mauled my tits as he picked up speed. It was obvious I was there for his pleasure and he intended to take it.

Despite having made myself cum only a few minutes earlier, I could feel another orgasm rising in my body. Antoine was now grunting loudly and thrusting forcefully into my cunt. Each time his body hit my mound it sent waves of pleasure into my brain and down to my toes. Suddenly he put his arms under my knees and lifted them up to my shoulders. I could feel his cock reaching deeper and yet deeper. It felt wonderful. There's no other word to describe the intense flood of sensations enveloping my body.

As Antoine let out an enormous moan I exploded into orgasm. My body vibrated with unbelievably powerful shockwaves that made me scream in pure ecstasy. I had never, ever had such an incredible orgasm in my life. The vibrations lasted for several minutes, their intensity diminishing slowly. I hardly noticed when Antoine dropped my legs and collapsed on top of me. His tongue found mine and we kissed passionately as I wound down from the amazing high I had just reached.

As I lay on the rock recovering from my exertions, Antoine pulled his cock out of my cunt with a loud plop. I could feel his cum dribbling down my crack. He had a huge smirk on his face as he knelt over my chest with his limp cock dangling in front of my face. His balls were tickling my chest. From this angle his dick looked massive. The foreskin was still pulled back and the swollen head was covered in Antoine's spunk and my juices.

Without a word Antoine pushed it towards my lips. My tongue automatically licked the tip and as he lowered his cock further I took it into my mouth and sucked on it with more energy than I expected. I sucked and licked and swallowed until his thick tool was clean.

It was only as Antoine jumped down from the rock that I remembered we had an audience. Any embarrassment I might have had had long disappeared as I lay in the sun, depleted after what had been the most memorable fuck of my life.

My legs were splayed and I knew my cunt lips were probably red and swollen from the pounding. Just as I was thinking that my darling husband would probably love to see my well-used cunt, Antoine took a picture of me.

"Just a quick one for her husband, I'm sending it now. I'll mark it 'one down'" Antoine said to his friends with a laugh.

Only the girl had changed position. She was still fully clothed, but was pointing a video camera at our little group. The two men seem to have been transfixed by the sight before them.

Now the blonde guy moved closer to the rock and jumped up to land between my legs. I was quite amused when he proferred his hand. Leaning on my left elbow I shook his hand lightly and he introduced himself as Christophe.

"I'm Anne," I replied casually, as if we were meeting in a café rather than on a rock high above Aix with me lying naked ready to let him have me.

His cock was pointing straight up to his belly button. He was also uncut, but the foreskin was already pulled back revealing the purple glans. Pre-cum was seeping copiously from his cock.

I lay back down and put my hands once again behind my head and looked blondie in the eye.

"Fancy some sloppy seconds?" I quipped opening my legs wider as an invitation.

He clambered on top of me. While resting on his elbows and without even a kiss or tit fumble he slipped into my velvety cunt. I gasped with the shock. Putting my head back on the rug I put my hands behind Christophe's head and pulled his lips to mine. My tongue frenziedly sought out his and we kissed passionately while he fucked me.

It couldn't have been more than 10 strokes and less than a minute when he squealed in his own ecstasy and filled me with his thick wad of cum.

Less than 2 minutes after mounting the rock (and me) he was already standing next to Antoine with a smug grin on his face and a spent cock covered in our mingled juices, no doubt with some of Antoine's too.

"Well, Michel," Antoine said to the other friend slapping him on the back. "Go make her scream. She'll be really smooth now after two loads."

Michel hopped onto the rock. I was looking at him defiantly, but he kept his eyes on my tits. His cock wasn't a thick or as long as the other two, but he was circumcised. The glans was really dark and glistening with pre-cum. I felt like taking him in my mouth, but before I could make a move he grabbed me and rolled me over.

He pulled my ass upwards then spread my legs. He now leaned forward and grabbed my tits ready for the ride and began thrusting with his dick in an effort to find my gaping hole.

His cock slid in almost unnoticed. My cunt must have been so slick with all the spent cum.

The slickness didn't seem to affect him, in fact he seemed to grow bigger inside me, and in doggy position he could reach my deepest spots.

As he pumped I rubbed my clitoris in rhythm with him.

My orgasm began to build quite quickly inside. As I rubbed my clit frantically and started my squeals, my third lover of the day let rip. As I felt his spunk hit my cervix, my orgasm intensified and my legs gave way. We both fell in a heap onto the rug.

Michel extricated himself from my body and bent down to place a chaste kiss on my cheek. He whispered a simple "thank you" into my ear, before climbing down from the rock.

I was spent. Utterly and absolutely. I lay on the rug with my eyes closed for a time. I heard talking in the background, but was oblivious to it.

When I sat up, the others were dressed and sitting on the ground in the shade around a bottle of wine. Antoine noticed my movement and called me over to join them.

I stepped gingerly off the rock, still in my heels, and walked as if on a catwalk the 20 or so yards to be with them. I felt rather naked with them all fully dressed, but didn't intend to beg for my clothes.

Antoine passed me a full glass of sparkling rosé and I gulped down half the glass immediately. I also grabbed a piece of bread with a hefty hunk of local cheese and gobbled it down. I was famished.

We all chatted pleasantly for half an hour or so, before Antoine's three friends said they were going to continue up the mountain and bade us goodbye.

The girl said her first words to me as they were leaving. "Anne, I'll edit the video and send you a copy. You are an extraordinarily sexy woman." As she said this she bent down and kissed me on the mouth. Her tongue darted past my lips for a moment and then the soft kiss was over. "Ciao, I hope we meet again," she breathed at me as she got up to leave.

I didn't know what to say. I'd just been kissed on the lips by a woman for the first time in my life and I didn't even know her name. From her accent I presumed she was Italian. From her kiss, I knew she had had an effect on me.

"Ciao Giuliana," Antoine said waving.

At least I knew her name now.

Antoine didn't seem to notice my discomfit as he tidied up the glasses and food. He then went to fetch the rug and packed everything in the basket.

When he was done, he took my hand and pulled me up.

"Let's text your husband, before we leave," he said winking, "What would he like to hear? Mm, let's see," he said, handing me the phone, "Write this: 'Cunt full of spunk. Three deposits all for you! Looking forward to sucking off Antoine in the car. Your naughty wife has lost all her clothes too. Home soon'."

I sent the message chuckling to myself. "So Antoine wants a blowjob does he. Randy old bugger," I thought to myself.

We walked slowly down the slope towards the car. I'd actually forgotten I was naked until a couple of hikers happened upon us as we came out of a clump of trees. They were both about 20, looked like students. As they drank in my nudity I checked out the lumps in their trousers. As we passed, Antoine and I both said hello, but didn't stop. They continued to stare after us until we disappeared from view (I couldn't help peaking behind a few times, to make sure they were watching my naked body. how vain I'd become!)

We reached the car in double quick time. I was becoming quite proficient at negotiating the rocky path in my heels. Once in the car, it was only a short drive back to Aix. I felt like we'd been away for days, but it had only been a few hours.

Antoine pulled up outside our villa. He still hadn't given me my clothes. I had found my bra on the seat where I had chucked it, but I had no idea where my dress and thong were now.

"Before you go, my lovely, you have something to take care of." As he said it he opened his trousers and let out his erection.

I knelt on the seat and bent over the gear stick to take him in my mouth. It wasn't the most comfortable position, but Antoine probably didn't mind.

His moans and groans began almost the moment I wrapped my lips around the tip. I licked off the pre-cum and made a noise of swallowing it, then began to bob up and down along his shaft.

As I did, I counted the strokes. Could I do it in under fifty, I mused. I wasn't sure how quickly a man of his age could recover.

I had reached 22 when the first spurt hit the back of my throat. I put up my tongue to catch the next big flood into my mouth and let it dribble out and down his cock. I kept sucking and stroking until he was spunked out. I lifted my face off his cock and looked at him. I put out my tongue, like I'd seen porn stars do, to show the result of my efforts, then swallowed it down for him.

My lips were still covered in thick goo, though.

"Now, get inside and give your husband a creamy kiss," he said, spanking me hard across the bottom. I grabbed my bra, phone and purse then stepped out of the car.

"Don't forget this," shouted Antoine as I moved towards the villa. He threw my dress at me. "Wear it tonight. Just that and heels for The Club. I'll pick you both up at 8:00."

As I went to open the door, Matt opened it and took me in his arms.

"My God, Anne, what a day. Shit, you're still naked. Look, I'm so sorry, I know, I should have rejected his proposals straight away. Are you all right? God you look so sexy."

As he rambled on he picked me up and carried me into the bedroom, slamming the front door shut behind him with his foot. Once he had placed me carefully on the bed he kissed me gently on the lips and no doubt savored the last remnants of Antoine's cum.

"Oh, Anne, I love you so much. I was so worried, but so turned on by all your messages. Did you really fuck three men? Really?"

I looked my husband of 15 years in the eyes and said, "Matt, today I had the best fuck I have ever had. I have never cum so strongly. Then two of Antoine's friends had their way with me and filled up my cunt with their spunk. Here, have a look," I said, opening my legs for him to have a good look at my well-worn cunt lips.

He moved back slightly to take in my body.

"You're tits are covered in red marks and scratches and your pussy, well it looks well used. It's so red and swollen. Let me kiss it for you…"

"Careful," I said, "it's a bit sensitive."

Matt kissed me tenderly on the thighs and round my mound, before moving towards my labia. No doubt he could taste my three lovers, but he said nothing. His kisses were soothing, but I was too exhausted for anything else and told him to come and cuddle up with me.

As he moved up my body to cuddle, I pulled the sheet over us and almost instantly I fell into a deep sleep leaving Matt to ponder on his slut wife.

4-3. Club Night - *Anne's Diary*

I didn't wake up until about 6:00 in the evening. As I rolled onto my back and stretched I saw Matt sitting on the sofa looking at me. Once he saw me open my eyes, he came over to me and kissed me.

For the next half hour he had me recount all that had happened that day in the hills. He wanted every detail. So, I left nothing out - it was his fantasy I was living after all. I sensed his hurt when I once again described my best fuck ever, but when I said it had been filmed those feelings rapidly gave way to voyeuristic lust.

"Where is the film? Can I see it?"

"No idea," I said. "A lovely girl called Giuliana was holding the camera. She took it with her up the mountain. That's all I know," I told him.

He looked disappointed.

"Don't worry," I said, "you'll have more memories for your fantasy chest tonight at The Club."

He was incredulous. "Tonight, already? Where, when, what do we have to do?"

I jumped up and moved towards the bathroom.

"Antoine's coming to get us at eight. Hurry along and make us something to eat while I have a long shower. I want to look my best for later, don't I?"

I spent at least half an hour just enjoying my shower. Besides having a lovely soak, I also touched up my legs and pussy, removing the tiny stubble that had begun to show through. I noticed too that I had caught a touch of sun during the day. My tits were a bit red, so I covered them in aloe vera to reduce the effect of the burn.

Matt, like the good husband he is, had whipped up a pasta carbonara, one of my favorite dishes and had poured me a delicious red to go with it.

I ate in silence, while Matt sat watching me. He was desperate to say something, but just couldn't get it said.

When I'd finished, I thanked him and went to get dressed. We only had about 30 minutes until Antoine came to pick us up.

A touch of mascara, some light lip gloss and a quick spray of Sally Hansen on my face and cleavage was all it took. I squirted on a hint of Lolita Lempicka in all the right places, pulled on my floral dress, stepped into my leopard skin heels and I was ready. "Life's a lot easier as a slut," I chuckled to myself.

Matt had put on a suit and tie and looked every inch the respectable businessman.

He didn't say anything when I made my entrance, just looked at his watch and said, "We should be off."

As he was opening the door, he turned to me.

"Anne," he said, "we really don't have to do this you know."

"I know, but I want to," I replied moving past him and out of the door.

At the kerb there was a black limo waiting. As I approached, the chauffeur dashed round to open the door for me. I stepped in.

Antoine greeted me with a four cheek kiss and drew me to sit next to him.

A few minutes later Matt followed me into the limo and the driver shut the door after him. Matt nodded to Antoine and sat opposite us with his back to the driver.

As we pulled away, Antoine opened a bottle of champagne and poured three glasses handing one to Matt and me.

"Anne," Antoine began, "I admire you and desire you. Once again you look absolutely gorgeous. You are a very lucky man, Matt. So let's drink to Matt, for sharing such beauty."

"To Matt," I said, clinking glasses with them both.

Matt smiled weakly and emptied his glass.

To my surprise we actually drove away from Aix towards Pertuis and then turned off onto a small road about 10 miles from the town.

Antoine was the perfect host during the drive. He chatted amiably, filled our glasses, opened a second bottle and flirted with me incessantly. His hand was constantly on my thigh when he wasn't busy with the champagne. Matt had noticed, of course, but said nothing.

After about 5 minutes on a small country road, we turned through some majestic gates onto a driveway. The gates closed automatically behind us and in the distance we could see the lights of a large country house.

The limo pulled up ay the front door and someone from the house stepped out to open the door for us.

"Good Evening, Master Antoine," he said formally as Antoine stepped out.

Antoine held out his hand for me and I stepped out of the limo followed by Matt.

The house was a typical Provencal *Bastide*, we'd probably call it a mansion. It was on a slight hill, so no doubt there would be great views across Provence during the daytime.

Antoine led me by the arm through the open door.

"This is so immaculately decorated," I thought.

I turned and motioned to Matt to catch up. When he was next to me, I took both my husband's and Antoine's arms and walked between into a large room full of rather elegantly dressed men and women. The men were mainly in suits, the women in cocktail dresses or, in some cases, long flowing evening dresses. My little floral number seemed a little understated.

From across the room I could see Master Pascal, my lover from last night, approaching us. He shook Matt's hand warmly, nodded to Antoine, then kissed me twice on each cheek like an old friend.

"This way my darling," he said to me. "Look after her husband, Antoine," he continued as he grabbed my hand and led me across the room leaving Antoine and Matt behind.

"You look just perfect for our little soirée. Let me get you some champagne and then the evening can begin."

A server handed me a glass of bubbly and I took a sip. I looked around the room. Everybody looked rather normal. I wasn't sure what I was expecting, but at the moment I felt like I was at a business convention.

"So what happens this evening?" I enquired of my host.

"Hasn't Antoine told you, most remiss of him. Well, as a supplicant, you will be presented and inspected, then our members will review your application. "

"Inspected?" I looked at him puzzled.

"Yes, my dear, all the members will inspect you and decide if you are worthy of membership. And then, if you pass the inspection and your review is satisfactory you will be granted honorary membership and be eligible to spend the night in one of our pleasure rooms. You will…"

I cut him off, "And Matt, my husband, will he be inspected?"

"Oh no, my dear, we only inspect the lady members. Should you be accepted, your husband will automatically become a consort member."

"Lucky him," I said with a straight face.

"Indeed," Master Pascal replied, totally missing my sarcasm.

"And will my husband be able to enjoy the pleasure rooms?"

"Absolutely not, unless he has an invitation from one of our members. Consorts are here merely to witness the pleasures of their wives. Consorts are held in the highest esteem. Any man who savors the spectacle of other men giving their wife pleasure is truly special."

"You can say that again," I said, knocking back yet another glass of bubbly.

"It is for that reason the club's official name is 'The Consort

Club'."

I look at him incredulously. Until a few days ago I had been amazed that my husband fantasized about me dressing in sexy clothes and showing me off to other men. Now, I was being introduced to a club where men willingly donated their wives so that other men could enjoy them both visually and physically. Now I knew why we had been selected, Matt was the ideal husband. Although, he didn't look too happy when I spied him across the room talking to Antoine and someone who looked like Christophe - blondie from the rock with the long cock. "They should have called it The Cuckold Club," I chuckled to myself. The champagne was making me tipsy.

Master Pascal took me by the arm and led me to a small stage at the end of the room. It was about four feet high and meant we were both visible to the whole room when we stood on it. It also meant I could get a better look at the members and consorts. I was wondering how to distinguish a consort from a member. The men were all dressed in suits and they didn't seem to have any badges or similar. I wondered if I could tell from the women they were with…

I was awoken from my reverie by Master Pascal's loud exhortation for everyone to approach the stage. Within seconds of speaking the room fell silent and all eyes fell on me and Master Pascal. I looked over at my husband and gave him a wink and a smile. He smiled weakly in reply and took a nervous sip of his champagne.

"Honored members, consorts and supplicant," he began, "tonight we are delighted to have a new supplicant," he continued looking at me, "as you can see she has all the attributes we demand of our supplicants. I should now like to invite her husband to join us on the stage. Please show your appreciation for Matt."

The crowd applauded and waited for Matt to go up on the stage. Antoine led my husband to the steps and urged him up. Matt was looking a little shy. His French was good, but I'm not sure he knew exactly what was happening.

As he stepped onto the stage the crowd's applause intensified. Matt walked self-consciously across to where I was standing with Master Pascal. Master Pascal took Matt's glass and place it to the side. He then shook his hand and congratulated him on having such a delightful wife and for choosing to join The Club.

Master Pascal now spoke to the audience again and explained what was going to happen, so that Matt wouldn't be left in the dark.

"So, Matt," Master Pascal said turning to my husband, "would you please prepare your wife for the inspection."

Matt and I looked at him mystified.

Master Pascal went on, "the husband will now remove his wife's apparel and in doing so confirm that he wishes to be a Consort of The Club."

Matt looked at me, "Do you really want this?" he whispered.

I knew at that moment I could have just left with Matt and we could have continued our lives, probably not quite as before, but along similar lines. I also knew that I had come too far in the last few days not to do this. Originally I had been doing it for Matt, now I was doing it for me. I couldn't explain exactly why, I just knew I had to do it.

"Do it," I said and handed my glass to Pascal. "Stuff the master crap," I thought, he's just a lecherous young man who likes fucking other men's wives.

Matt came and stood in front of me and went to undo the straps around my neck.

"Not like that, do it properly from behind," I scolded him, "make a show of it, do it slowly and seductively."

Matt stepped behind me and I looked down at the sea of eyes staring up at me. With the straps undone Matt slowly pulled down the front of my dress. As my nipples came into view I heard a few mutterings from the crowd, no doubt remarking how pointed and stiff they were. I was wondering now whether Matt would drop my dress to my feet or pull it off over my head. Men seemed to always go the feet route.

Surprise, surprise, slowly Matt lifted the skirt portion of the dress upwards. Very soon my bald cunt would be visible to everyone. I was hot and wet at the thought. My nipples were so hard.

As my cunt lips were revealed the crowd clapped and Matt pulled my dress completely off over my head.

I was now standing on a stage in nothing but my favorite heels in front of thirty or so strangers.

Pascal now took me by the hand to the back of the stage. On the wall were some restraints. He lifted my left arm over my head and wrapped one round my wrist followed by my right. Now he pulled my left leg to the side and strapped me to the wall by the ankle. He then did the same to the right ankle. I was now spreadeagled upright on the stage. A spotlight was turned on to highlight me against the dark backdrop. Matt was being led to a chair at the edge of the stage. I tried to look him in the eye, but he was looking at the floor.

"Members, your supplicant is ready for inspection." Pascal motioned the members to come onto the stage.

"At least I'll know who the consorts are," sprang to mind.

The members, both male and female formed an orderly line and approached me singly and occasionally in pairs.

Many of them nodded a friendly "bonsoir" and just passed on by, after looking me up and down. But some were bolder and took hold of my breasts and fondled my nipples or ran their hands up and down my legs, across my cunt lips and over my upper body.

One man kissed me on the lips and stuck his tongue roughly into my mouth. At the same time he pushed two fingers unceremoniously into my sopping cunt. He then lifted his fingers to his nose, took in my aroma and then popped them into his mouth, savouring the flavor like a good wine. A couple of others also invaded my cunt, some fingered my clit. Most of the women merely kissed me on the cheek and congratulated me. I wasn't sure for what, but thanked them anyway.

Antoine was the last member to approach me with Christophe at his side. They both kissed me chastely and congratulated me.

With all the clit rubbing and cunt fondling I was well on my way to orgasm and wondered if that would be part of the show.

Pascal came to undo me and walked me to the edge of the stage.

"Congratulations to the supplicant," he said, "she has passed the inspection."

4-4. Member's Benefits - *Anne's Diary*

Pascal now took me to sit next to my husband who hadn't moved during the inspection ordeal.

As I sat down, I leaned over and kissed him on the lips. He kissed me back and took me by surprise when he said, "Thank you, you are incredible."

I didn't have time to reply as Pascal now called the crowd to order and announced the commencement of the review.

The lights dimmed and a large screen dropped down at the back of the stage. I looked at Matt. He was staring intently at the screen. I looked up and realized why. On the screen was our bedroom. Pascal was sitting on the sofa and Matt was moving towards the ensuite door as I appeared through it.

"How on earth? They filmed us at home."

Matt was entranced by the scene unfolding on the screen although he already knew what was going to happen.

Very soon it became obvious that the sound quality was excellent and that there had been three cameras in the room. Someone had done a great job of editing.

I had rarely seen myself on the screen and I had definitely never seen myself being fucked.

As a porno film it wasn't bad. Quite arousing, I thought. I

noticed that I was now rubbing myself between my legs as Pascal thrust his cock in my mouth on the screen.

The crowd cheered when Pascal filled my mouth with his cum.

I took hold of Matt's hand when Pascal began fucking me on the bed, in anticipation of seeing my husband clean off another man's prick. I was getting very aroused watching it. It was almost impossible to associate the lustful images on the screen with me and Matt.

The crowd cheered even louder when Matt took a mouthful of Pascal's spunk.

Then, when Pascal made me present my gaping asshole to him and took me in the ass there was a ripple of pleasure through our audience. I felt more than a tingle as he penetrated me. Seeing myself presenting my willing hole was sending me over the edge.

I let go of Matt's hand and felt how hard he had become. Despite his demeanor, he was enjoying our performance.

The movie faded to a close as we cuddled in bed. "How romantic," I thought, "Very unpornolike."

I was relieved it was over and wondered whether my review had passed muster.

But, the movie hadn't ended. Cut to a mountainside.

"Oh, shit, no…, that's why they filmed it today," I said out loud to no one in particular, but Matt heard and grasped my hand again. Now he'd get to see my best fuck ever.

"Is this, you know, you, today…?" he asked.

"I reckon so," I said. "Now you'll get to witness my best ever fuck. Well, at least it's been preserved for posterity, we'll have something to show our grandchildren."

My attempt at levity fell on deaf ears, as Matt was riveted to the screen and the erotic view of his wife with legs splayed lying naked on a rock.

It was obvious the video camera was hand-held, but the quality was no less good than the earlier part of the movie. Giuliana had done a great job. I looked quite stunning, even though I said so myself. Just before Antoine started to fuck me, she had zoomed in on my obviously wet cunt and panned up to show my face as Antoine knelt between my legs with his dick ready to plunge into me.

As Antoine thrust his thick cock into my ready and willing cunt, I was captivated. The audience was silent, watching every move. Out of the corner of my eye I spotted my husband playing with his dick. He had released it from his trousers and was now openly rubbing it. I suppose I should take it as a compliment that my own husband found me sufficiently erotic to want to wank himself off to images of me on the screen.

As Antoine and I reached our climax in the movie, Matt's

throaty grunts told me he was close to coming, so I knelt down in front of him and took his cock in my mouth. He sighed with pleasure as my lips enfolded him. My orgasmic cries on the screen were reaching their crescendo so I speeded up my movement and brought my husband to a screaming orgasm just as Antoine deposited his cum in me on film. No doubt Matt expected me to pull away at the last moment as I had always done before, but his Anne was no longer the Anne of old. I savored his thick jets of cum and swallowed them down as he ejaculated in my mouth.

When he was done, I licked him clean and gave him a passionate kiss on the mouth, just as Christian entered me on the rock.

I sat back down and continued to hold Matt's partially limp dick. Christophe and Michel cumming in me brought Matt's dick to life again, but the movie now came to an end and the lights came on again and the audience were clapping and cheering.

Matt turned away from the crowd and stuffed his cock back in his trousers. He needn't have been embarrassed, I spotted a few others doing the same in the audience.

Pascal came to front of the stage and beckoned me over to him. I'd forgotten I was still naked, but strode over to him with a haughty air.

"Congratulations, Anne, you are now an honorary member of The Club." The audience cheered and clapped at the news.

"In honor of your admission to our ranks you will be given the *Chambe de Sade* pleasure room tonight. It is the best we have to offer. Your consort," he looked across at Matt, "will have full audio and video access for his own voyeuristic enjoyment, should you allow it. The control buttons are in the headboard of the bed."

Pascal called Matt over to stand next to me.

"Members," Pascal continued, "What are you bid for the first night with our newest member? Who wishes to induct her into the delights of the *Chambre de Sade*?"

"You mean they're going to pay to fuck me?" I looked at Pascal.

"Not exactly, they're going to pay to enjoy you for the next 12 hours or so in a pleasure room. Whether you fuck or not is irrelevant."

"10,000," came a shout from the floor.

"And who gets this money," I asked.

"It goes to local children's charities, Pascal replied. We are major sponsors of children's charities in the area.

"15,000."

"20,000"

"25,000"

I was in shock, someone was willing to pay 25,000 euros to fuck me, are they nuts?

Then a voice I recognized shouted from the back, "100,000 euros."

There was a rumble of surprise in the crowd as heads turned to see who had made the bid. "Well fuck me," I thought, "it was Christophe, my fuck-buddy from this morning. Why does he want to pay so much to have me again? He only lasted 2 minutes this morning."

Pascal declared the bidding closed when no further bids were forthcoming. One of the servers stepped out from the back of the stage and indicated he wanted me to follow him. Pascal kissed me on both cheeks, congratulated me again and wished me an erotic evening. I turned to look at Matt, but Pascal quickly said, "Not to worry, my darling, we will show your consort the way." Matt smiled at me and gave a small wave. I waved back and blew him a kiss.

The crowd clapped and cheered as I left the stage and followed the server into the depths of the house.

We went down several sumptuously decorated corridors before arriving at double oak doors. The servant opened both doors ceremoniously and let me in to a beautiful spacious bedroom. As I entered he bade me good evening and closed the doors behind me.

The bed was round and huge. It could have fit at least 10 people sleeping side by side. The ceiling and walls were replete with mirrors. I opened the doors that led off on each side of the bed. One led to a massive ensuite with hot tub, bath, showers, massage tables and all sorts of other contraptions I had never seen before and a huge shelf full of make-up, perfumes, powders, gels and oils.

The other door led to a walk-in closet filled with male and female costumes, lingerie, sex toys, ropes and chains, and umpteen other drawers and cupboard full of all sorts.

I picked out a satin kimono and put it on. I already felt more comfortable wearing something, even alone.

Still no sign of Christophe. I was feeling good about myself in the knowledge that a young man was willing to pay obscene money to spend a night with me, particularly as he had already had the pleasure of me once.

"He must have enjoyed himself," I said out loud to myself chuckling.

Back in the main room, I checked out the cameras in each corner of the ceiling and also in the walls at eye level. A total of eight cameras in all. As Pascal had said there was a control panel in the headboard. I was able to stream the feed externally or stream it internally. or turn it off completely. It was already off, so I turned it to stream internally. Within about 10 seconds of flicking the switch a panel in the wall by the door opened to reveal 8 screens - one for each camera I rapidly determined, for there I was duplicated 8 times from different angles. I pulled the remote from the headboard panel and pressed a few switches.

"Very impressive," I thought, I could set all eight screens to act as one from any of the cameras I selected. I could pan and zoom. This was perfect for making a porno movie. I hadn't yet decided whether I wanted to turn on external streaming tonight. Perhaps I should go for just audio and give Matt a tantalizing night as he tries to imagine what's happening to me.

As I put the remote down on the bed, I spotted a door hidden in left-hand wall. Behind it was a fridge stocked with a large selection of drinks, hors d'oeuvres, fruit and other delicacies. Next to the fridge was a cupboard full of snacks, chocolates, nuts and the like.

The furniture dotted here and there around the room was made up of standard armchairs, a couple of sofas and various other strange looking love seats, benches and other peculiarly shaped objects. Most of the pieces had hooks and stuff for constraining and as I looked more closely I realized that there were hooks and chains in various places around the room.

Before I had time to explore further there was a discreet knock at the door.

"Come in, Christophe." I shouted.

I stood up and moved towards the door to greet him, I had

decided I was going to make this a truly memorable night for him.

Christophe was good looking, fit and, more importantly, had an impressive cock. But most of all, anyone willing to pay 100,000€ for me deserved the best and it would definitely last longer than the two minutes we'd had on the rock.

PART FIVE
Cam Control

5-1. Wife Voyeur

As my wife was led away by one of the servers, our neighbor Antoine came up to me.

"Congratulations," he said jovially, "it takes a very special person to be a consort. You must be so proud of your beautiful, sexy wife."

I had to admit in many ways I was proud. I had to also admit that I would never have dreamed a week ago that my obsessive fantasy to reveal my wife to others would bring us here, to a club dedicated to those who reveled in such fantasies and made such fantasies so blindingly real.

A few days ago, to my delight at the time, I had unleashed the power of her "inner slut" (as, in my ignorance, I called it), but I was now struggling to come to terms with my own feelings of inadequacy. It had all happened so fast. We hadn't really had time to talk about anything. I could see that Anne had discovered a power from the pleasures of her own sexy body. Watching my wife offering her naked body to others was so incredibly arousing. Seeing her being taken by another man was so indescribably erotic. So why wasn't I happy for her and for me?

My thoughts were disturbed by Antoine, "Let me show you to the viewing room," he said. "You will love it. There is everything you need to enjoy your wife's adventures."

So saying, he led me off the stage and down a long corridor to what looked like a bedroom. It was rather luxurious. On the wall opposite the king size bed there was one huge screen with eight smaller screens arranged in two rows next to it. On all the screens I could see Anne, wearing what looked like a kimono, in some large bedroom. She seemed to be alone and was moving around the room looking in cupboards and drawers and generally having a good look round.

Antoine told me to make myself comfortable.

"The hostess will be with you soon to provide absolutely anything you require. The room is yours for the night. Enjoy your wife's adventures, enjoy your hostess."

With that he left, closing the door behind him. I took off my jacket and tie and flung them over the back of a chair. The remote for the screens was on the bedside table. I picked it up and tried out some of the buttons. Quite an impressive system. I was able to swap the camera angle for the big screen, pan with each camera and even zoom. The audio seemed to be working, because I could clearly hear the clunk of cupboards and doors opening, but Anne hadn't yet spoken, so I had no idea how well it would catch speech.

I watched my darling wife lovingly as she moved about the room. She looked stunning in the silk kimono. Sitting here watching her like this I wasn't feeling jealousy or inadequacy, I was feeling lust.

"It's all a matter of trust," I said to myself, "I love her and I know she loves me. I love watching her fucking other men, I love seeing her show her body to other men. But most of all I know she will come home. That's the issue. So instead of moping about, enjoy your beautiful wife and her adventure tonight."

My little pep talk to myself boosted my spirits. I shimmied up the bed and made myself comfortable with the trusty remote in hand. "What could be better than a porn movie starring your own wife," I chuckled to myself and felt my dick growing hard in my pants.

As I was having fun zooming in on my wife and trying out all the fancy tricks you could do with the cameras and screens, a rather fetching young girl walked into my room carrying a tray. I jumped up in surprise, feeling as if I'd been caught doing something I shouldn't.

"Monsieur, I am your hostess for the night. I brought you some champagne, but if you prefer there is wine and beer in the fridge over here," she said, pointing to a fridge built into the wall that I hadn't noticed. She placed the tray next to me on the bedside table and proffered a glass of champagne.

I took the glass and looked at the girl. She was wearing a similar silk kimono to the one my wife had on. Her dark hair was long, reaching down over one shoulder to her breasts. She looked Asian. Her face was exquisite. It was one of those faces you just want to look at because it is so beautiful.

"My name is Ly," she said in French, "but if you prefer," she continued in English, "we can talk English."

She picked up a glass of champagne from the tray, "If I may?"

"Of course, please do." I said, "I do apologize, I was lost in my thoughts when you came in. And yes, I prefer English, if that's ok."

She looked me in the eyes and clinked glasses.

"To an erotic adventure," she said enigmatically.

"Er, yes, absolutely," I replied, "To an erotic adventure."

We drank in silence for a moment.

"Please, sit," she said. "I want to make you comfortable."

I did as she asked, climbing back onto the bed next to the remote.

"So that beautiful woman is you wife?" Ly asked, pointing to the screen.

"Yes, she is," I said, "And yes, she is very beautiful. So are you," I said.

To my surprise Ly blushed and clinked glasses again. "Thank you."

Ly went over to the door and clicked the lock into place.

"That will give us a little more privacy," she said. "There are no cameras in this room, only in the members' pleasure rooms. We tell the members they can turn off the camera feed, but they can't, you know. Consorts can have uninterrupted coverage of their wife's erotic adventure." Ly came back over to the bed and asked if she could sit next to me.

"Do you want me to take off my robe now?" she asked.

I told her there was no need and that I would love her to sit next to me.

She shuffled up close to me - close enough for me to inhale her lovely scent - and she linked her arm through mine.

"So what's she up to, this gorgeous wife of yours?" she asked.

"Nothing much really," I replied. "She seems to be checking out the room. I think she's alone, since I can't see anybody else in range of the cameras." Ly snuggled into my body and looked up at me.

"Don't worry, she'll soon have a companion. I presume that's why you're here."

"Well, yes, I suppose so," I said, "but…"

"Please, you don't have to explain. Tonight you can watch the cam for as long as you want. You can turn off the video feed or sound feed, or even both as you wish."

"And you, Ly, will you watch my wife's adventures with me?"

"If that's what you desire, Sir. I am here for you. Whatever you desire, I will provide."

I looked at her intrigued. "Absolutely anything?"

"Of course. We look after our consorts. I am yours until morning."

5-2. Italian Surprise - *Anne's Diary continues…*

I was rather enjoying my exploration of the *Chambre de Sade* - the reason for the name had become somewhat obvious within minutes of my arrival - and I had quite forgotten why I was there.

The discreet knock at the door brought me back to reality.

"Come in, Christophe." I shouted.

I moved towards the door to greet him, I had decided I was going to make this a truly memorable night for him since Christophe, who had already had a brief encounter with my cuntly delights today, was good looking, fit and, more importantly, had an impressive cock. However, what impressed me the most was that he had been willing to bid 100,000€ for me in The Club auction, not 15 minutes ago. He deserved the best and it would definitely last longer than the two minutes of in-out sex we'd had that morning high in the hills above Aix.

"Ciao, Cara"

"What the…! How did you get here, Giuliana?" I ran to her and hugged her like a long lost friend.

"Just a minute," she said, "let me put my bag down."

She dropped it at her feet, turned to bolt the door, then turned back to face me. She moved close to me, took my face in her hand and kissed me with intense passion on the lips. Her tongue sought out mine and I couldn't help but respond in kind.

My kimono came undone as we kissed which allowed Giuliana the chance to run her hands over my body. Her hands felt soft and warm as she caressed my stomach, moving her hands sensually up towards my breasts. She cupped my left breast and ever so slightly tweaked my nipple with her finger and thumb. My knees gave way as she did and we broke off our kiss.

I sat back on the bed and pulled my kimono tight around me and looked at Giuliana.

She was wearing the same clothes as this morning on the mountain: jeans, a loose t-shirt and a pair of black elasticated tai-chi shoes. Her hair was long, dyed blonde (her dark eyebrows gave her away) and tied up haphazardly with a pin at the back leaving a fair amount of hair overflowing over the pin. The hair that flowed over the pin cascaded downwards and bounced as she moved. I loved the look.

I could see us both on the screen by the door as I looked past Giuliana. As I saw us, I grabbed the remote and made sure I had turned off the remote streaming of both audio and video. I wasn't sure I wanted Matt to hear or see this. For some reason, this felt different. This wasn't part of Matt's sexual fantasy to my mind.

Giuliana fetched her bag from by the door and sat next to me on the bed. She looked into the bag and pulled out a bundle of video camera tapes and DVDs.

"Your movies," she said. "I took the originals and all the copies. They're all here. You can do what you want with them, but I didn't want others to get hold of them."

"How did you do that?" I asked, feeling huge relief at getting control of the movies.

"I do all the video production and editing for this club," she said. "That's why I was on the mountain this morning, Antoine had told us to be there."

"Told you? When?" I looked at her in shock.

"Yesterday evening, when I was editing your session with Pascal."

"But, how did he know I'd accept?"

"You did, didn't you? Antoine can be very persuasive and you'd already been softened by Pascal's smooth control the night before."

"And you edit these movies? Did you install the cameras in our bedroom too?"

"Yes, I did. Sorry. I hadn't met you then, it was just a job. Pascal gave me the instructions a couple of days ago. I had plenty of time when you went out for the day."

"I can't believe it. Do you do this often?"

"Well, not often, once a month probably. It's not my full time job, I'm actually an independent filmmaker, this is just how I pay the bills. I'm really sorry, believe me."

"Giuliana, I really don't mind that you filmed me, not now that I've seen how good you made me look," I laughed and touched her arm, "And now that you're giving me the originals, I couldn't be happier. Won't The Club be upset with you?"

"I don't care," she said defiantly, "I'm not doing this any more. Meeting you made me see sense. I should thank you."

She touched my face lovingly with her hand and leaned over to kiss me on the lips again.

I pulled back, "Wait, just a minute, Giuliana, I'm not lesbian, you know, I'm… I'm… well I'm just not sure."

"Forgive me, I was attracted to you as soon as I saw you when I was editing your movie with Pascal. I wouldn't call myself lesbian either, I go for both boys and girls. Somehow I thought you felt something for me. I felt it in your kiss on the mountain. You definitely felt something, didn't you?"

I was very confused.

"Yes, I had felt something, I admitted. "I'm feeling something now and I was really pleased to see you when you came in just now. So much has happened in the last few days, that I don't really know what I feel at all."

As I spoke she took my hand and looked into my eyes. I leaned over and kissed her on the lips. She responded passionately and we rolled back onto the bed scattering the tapes and DVDs as we locked lips.

We lay next to each other looking into each other's eyes. I put my hand on Giuliana's cheek and caressed her soft skin. It suddenly occurred to me that Christophe would be appearing soon.

"What about Christophe? He just paid a pile of money to have me for the night. Where is he?"

"Don't worry, cara mia," Giuliana replied soothingly. He made the bid for me. We've got all night and as much time as you want thereafter.

"You paid 100,000€ for a night with me? You must be nuts…"

"Well actually I didn't, I don't have that kind of money, but Christophe does. He's stinking rich and madly in love with me, but he knows we'll never be a couple. It just wouldn't work. I told him that I'd fallen head over heels in love with you and…"

"In love? With me? But…"

"Yes, I know, it's a bit sudden, but for the last day or so I've been watching you intimately and feel I know you rather well. When we met in person, I felt even more for you. But anyhow, Christophe gifted me this night. He's a romantic at heart and would do anything for me, I'm so lucky."

She kissed me again and pulled me close to her. I was in a daze. There was definitely something between us, it's just I'd never even imagined kissing a woman, let alone loving one. But, talking about never imagining, I would never have imagined being fucked in all my holes by a stranger. Even more unimaginable would have been a scene with my husband cheering him on. So what the fuck, I could at least go with the flow. And I really did like Giuliana. And if I was honest, I'd have to say I was attracted to her.

"Look, Anne, there's a massage table here with all sorts of scented oils, let me give you a massage. Then when you're nice and relaxed we can cuddle up in bed, drink some wine and enjoy the food they've laid on. Let's just have a girls' night in. How does that sound?"

"Sounds lovely. When you've done me, I can massage you too, if you like."

"Done. I'll go put on a kimono too and get the oils ready. Why don't you make yourself comfortable on the table."

5-3. Lust at First Sight

Ly and I sat on the bed and enjoyed the champagne she'd brought. She was a delightful girl. We chatted about France, about Vietnam - she'd left there 10 years ago when she was 14 - and about The Club.

She explained that it was a part-time job, since The Club only met 2-3 times a month at most. But the short working hours and her decent pay from The Club meant she could study as a full-time student at the University in Aix. In another year she'd be a doctor and be able to leave The Club behind.

I was so taken by Ly and her story that I totally forgot about the events in the other room. As Ly went to fetch some more drinks from the fridge, I happened to glance at the screen and saw my wife lying on a bed kissing a woman. It was a quite a passionate kiss, they were definitely more than just friends.

Ly joined kneeled next to me on the bed with two beers as I reached for the remote to turn up the volume.

I was stunned. The woman was the one who had paid to spend the night with my wife and was now talking about being in love with Anne. I grabbed a beer off Ly and drank a good half of the bottle.

"Are you okay, Sir?" Ly asked, looking at me with a worried frown.

"No, it's just I've had a bit of a shock. It seems my wife's having an affair with a woman. She never said a word to me. It's been a funny few days, and now this, I'm bewildered."

As I turned towards Ly she kissed me on the lips. I put my arms around her and kissed her back forcefully. Her lips were soft and wet. I was heady from her scent.

I pulled away to put down my bottle and clicked the off button on the remote. "No need for a voyeur fantasy, I thought, "When I have such a stunner right here in my bed."

I turned back to Ly.

"Shall I take off my kimono, Sir?" she asked, looking at me with a demure smile.

"Please call me Matt," I said, "But let me help you with the kimono, I want to take it off you slowly."

Ly kneeled in front of me and let me do just that. I kissed her neck and slowly revealed her shoulders. As the silky kimono slid down her arms I took in the beauty of her superb breasts. She had delightful puffy nipples that were stiff and hard. Her breasts had no tan lines and were probably a B or small C cup. "Just perfect," I thought, as I kissed my way down to her left nipple and took it gently into my mouth.

Ly was moaning softly as I played with her nipple. My tongue circled it and I pulled and tweaked it with my teeth. I gently laid

Ly back on the bed and continued my exploration of her flawless body. With the kimono off her arms, she was now lying totally naked in front of me.

She looked at me invitingly as I kissed her open lips before moving down past her breasts, across her flat stomach and belly button ring, to her hairy mound. Still no tan lines. Her pubes were dark and thick. I loved them. As my lips moved over her mound she spread her legs to expose her glistening pussy. Despite the pubic hair, I could see her pink pussy lips; they were visibly engorged and ready for my tongue.

Instead of diving straight at her pussy (as Anne often complained I did), I moved down to her feet and massaged them and kissed them. Gradually I worked my way up each leg, kissing and stroking Ly until I reached her inner thighs. I could smell her arousal and gently ran my tongue around her pussy, avoiding the labia and clitoris. I swirled and licked, gradually moving onto her pussy lips. Ly moaned in ecstasy as my tongue caressed them. When my tongue penetrated her labia, her wetness flowed onto my tongue. I lapped it up and pushed my tongue in further. Ly's then sat up and pulled my head up to kiss her mouth.

"No, Matt, I'm here for you, let's get your clothes off, so I can play with you."

Ly began unbuttoning my shirt and pulling it off me. I had to stand up, wobbling on the bed, while we both got rid of my pants and Ly pulled down my boxers.

My cock felt so hard, even though I had cum only an hour or so earlier on stage during my wife's on-screen performance. When Ly licked the end of my cock and put her lips around it, I was close to erupting.

"You like that, don't you," she said stating the obvious, as she licked up and down my shaft and caressed my balls with her hands. She then placed her hands on my butt cheeks and took my cock into her mouth, using her hands to pump me back and forth all the while keeping her beautiful eyes focused on mine. Each time I watched my cock disappear into her mouth I felt a frisson of pleasure surge along my spine.

The moment was fast approaching and there was no way I could hold back. I put my hand on her head to feel her silky soft black hair.

"I'll be coming very soon," I said in a rather husky voice. The pleasures ripping through my body were affecting my ability to speak as well.

Ly's movements slowed and she went back to licking my glans softly. I groaned forcefully when her lips pulled away from my cock. She began fondling my balls with one hand and sought out my asshole with the other. As she swallowed my cock once more she jammed a finger into my ass. I jerked in shock as unexpected pleasure bursts radiated from my asshole through my dick and into my head. It was like a mini orgasm. My moans must have been very loud. Ly's eyes faithfully followed me and made the experience even stronger.

She now began fucking my dick with her mouth and lips. She didn't take me far inside her mouth, just enough to stimulate the ridge with her lips. The finger in my ass was now pumping vigorously.

"I'm cuuuu…. mmm…. iiiiing," I screamed as a jet of sperm erupted from my cock into her exquisite mouth. She used one set of fingers like a cock ring and restrained the flow somehow, causing explosions in my brain as the sperm was held back and released once more to explode in another massive jet. She had also pushed her finger deeply into my ass.

I can't be sure how long my orgasm lasted. Time stopped for me and this wonderful, beautiful, sexy woman who now pulled her finger from my ass, dropped my cock from her mouth and looked up at me with those adorable eyes. She opened her mouth and popped out her tongue. It was covered in my thick gooey spunk. As I bent down to kiss her she put her tongue back in her mouth and swallowed my gift down.

Our lips locked and we fell back onto the bed.

"Ly, you are the most wonderful woman I have ever met," I said in between kisses. I pulled her close and kissed her more. My hands were caressing her delicious puffy nipples that were growing even more as I touched them.

When my hands reached her pussy, my fingers slipped in easily. She was small and tight, but oh so slick with her own juices.

I began to move down her body, but she stopped me.

"No, Matt, you are my guest. If you want to pleasure me, just lie back and let me do the work."

I looked at her quizzically as she rolled me onto my back. Ly then straddled me around the head. I was looking up into her velvety pussy as she slowly lowered herself onto my eagerly waiting lips and tongue. Her juices were dribbling onto my tongue as I licked and slurped her pussy. Ly balanced herself by putting her hands on the wall above the bed and ground her pussy and clit on my tongue and lips. Her breathing began to quicken and she made small murmurs. The murmurs turned to screams as her grinding became wild and erratic, I had difficulty keeping my tongue in what I presumed was the right place. As her body shuddered and the screams reached a peak she moved her pussy down my body and collapsed onto my chest, kissing me with rapid kisses and saying, "thank you, thank you, thank you," over and over, before resting her head on my shoulder and falling into a deep sleep.

5-4. Escape to Reality - *Anne's Diary continues…*

Giuliana returned from the ensuite wearing a kimono like my own, carrying some oils in a basket. She pressed a button on the seat at the end of the bed. After a few whirrs and clicks, it magically turned into a massage table.

"Jump on," Giuliana said as she put the oil basket on the shelf built under the table.

I stood up and moved round the bed next to Giuliana ready to climb on the massage table. Giuliana kissed me again when I reached her and slipped my kimono of my shoulders. For some reason I was feeling embarrassed being naked in front of her.

We were still kissing as the kimono hit the floor. I now reached up to slide Giuliana's kimono from her body and stepped back to watch as it slipped down her body.

She was slightly shorter than me. Her breasts were bigger with enormous areolae. Probably because of their size they were slightly more pendulous than mine. Her tummy was flatter than mine though and, to my surprise, she had copious, dark pubic hair. I looked her up and down appreciatively.

"You are beautiful," I said. "Quite beautfiul."

She kissed me again and said, "Thank you. You are too, I adore your body."

I climbed onto the massage table and took my place on my stomach, putting my face through the hole and placing my arms by my side. I already felt very relaxed.

"I'll start with your shoulders and move down your back to your buttocks and then the back of your legs. Okay?" she asked.

"Absolutely any way you want," I said. "I am in your hands."

Giuliana poured some oil on my back. It was warm, I wasn't sure how she'd managed that, and smelled of Jasmine and another scent I couldn't place. She spread the oil over my back and then began massaging my shoulders.

Her touch was gentle, soft, but really effective. As she moved down my back I felt myself drifting off into pleasureland. When she reached my buttocks, she jumped down to my feet and began to work her way up my legs. She lifted each leg in turn, and after pouring on some oil she worked my calf muscle, before placing my leg softly back on to the table. Her fingers on the back of my thighs felt lovely. And as Giuliana moved from my thighs up to my buttocks my pussy was already responding to the sensations.

When she'd finished kneading my buttocks, Giuliana tapped me lightly on the bum and told me it was time to roll over.

I hesitated a second, but realized that embarrassment now was futile. Giuliana had watched me taking five cocks in various holes over the last couple of days and had seen me more naked than almost anyone I knew.

So, I flipped over. She adjusted the headrest to make me comfortable and poured some oil liberally on my breasts and stomach. It dribbled down my sides, into my belly button and down my crack - unimpeded by pubic hair.

Giuliana kissed me again with a quick flick of the tongue into my mouth and started on my stomach. She was a skilled masseuse. I was loving every minute of the massage. Her hands moved across my stomach and up to my breasts, just touching them a little. She did this movement several times, before moving up and round my breasts to my shoulders. She did this several times too, up to my shoulders around the outside of my breasts, just brushing them a little, then back down to my stomach between my breasts.

After a dozen or so similar strokes, I was longing for her to touch my breasts properly. She continued the light touching for a few more movements before taking both breasts into her hands from the underside. She squeezed them gently moving her fingers across them. Such ecstasy. I was now desperate for her to touch my nipples.

She squeezed a few more times then brushed her palms lightly across my rigid nipples. And then back again. I uttered a small moan when she touched them for the first time. She lightly stroked them several times before focusing on my left breast with both hands. She squeezed the breast from all sides with her hands and pulled her hands upwards until she was squeezing my nipples. As she reached the top, my breasts flopped back and I could start breathing again.

A dozen times like that on both breasts was sending me wild. And when she finally grabbed both my nipples forcefully between thumb and forefinger I squealed with pleasure. At that moment I was sure I could have a breast orgasm if she continued.

She kissed me softly after my squeal of pleasure and moved down to my legs. She lifted a couple of stirrups at the end of the table and placed my ankles in them. She then divided the bottom half of the massage table somehow and my legs were wide open.

Giuliana stepped between my legs and focused on my left leg. She oiled my foot, shin and thigh then massaged it all the way up, stopping excruciatingly close to my pussy.

She then did the same with my right leg. When she reached the top of the thigh she grabbed the oil and poured it onto my mound. I could feel the oil dribbling along my crack and over my labia.

From her position between my legs Giuliana was able to massage the tops of my thighs and my mound in comfort. Teasingly she rubbed me all over my mound without touching my pussy lips or clitoris. Slowly, slowly she pushed her thumbs up and over my outer lips. She did this several times.

My pussy was probably leaking profusely by now, my juices mixing in with the massage oil. As my pussy opened to her touch I could feel her touching my inner lips. Slowly, little by little she was penetrating my sopping wet pussy.

Giuliana now moved from between my legs. I let out a little cry in fear that she was stopping, but her fingers found me again from the side. She used her left hand to move her fingers up and down my crack. Her right hand she used to press down on my mound.

The sensations were unbelievable.

Suddenly she pushed he fingers into my willing pussy. I shrieked and made Giuliana laugh. She smiled at me and bent down to give me a chaste kiss on the nipple, before returning to her massage.

She now had two or three fingers plunging into me at speed. He right hand, on my mound, was pushing down and every so often she would flick my clitoris with her thumb.

The noises I was making in my throat were indescribable. The sensations in my pussy totally out of this world. I felt as if I was cumming, but not cumming. The sensations were too intense. Suddenly she began pushing her fingers even more vigorously into me, and then she stopped all of a sudden. My body went into shock, I needed those fingers in me.

"Please, please..." I entreated.

She smiled at me and plunged her fingers into me again. Her breasts jiggled as she forcefully moved her fingers in and out, before stopping again and removing them.

I shrieked again.

My body was beginning to shake uncontrollably. She plunged those divine fingers in again and with one thrust I came more forcefully than I could have imagined. My body was shaking and shuddering, my pussy muscles were in overdrive and suddenly a huge spurt of liquid gushed from between my legs. I'd squirted. I had never ever squirted. In fact, I didn't believe it possible to squirt.

But Giuliana didn't stop. She let the spasms and shuddering calm slightly, then plunged her fingers in again and moved them rapidly in and out. I could feel the shuddering begin to build again, then she stopped. She waited, looking at me. Without warning she started again vigorously and bang, I shuddered uncontrollably and once again I squirted. "The floor must be sopping wet," flashed through my mind, but I was shaking so much, I couldn't concentrate.

When Giuliana then shoved her fingers in again and did her rapid movements, I was begging for mercy, but within seconds the shuddering had started and I couldn't speak.

Giuliana held my pussy softly with her left hand and with her right hand she brushed the sweat and hair from my brow.

I was still feeling the aftershocks. My body was still jerking slightly, but I was calmer. As the final shudders ceased, Giuliana went and pulled back the covers of the bed, then came and picked me up off the massage table and carried me to the bed. She put me down gently and covered me with a sheet as she snuggled in beside me. I was still shaking slightly and I could still feel the orgasm all over my body. "How did she do that?" was all I could think, "What a woman!."

I managed to whisper a simple thank you to my unbelievable lover. She kissed me gently on the lips and cuddled me close. I kissed her back with the little energy I had, but soon my eyes closed and I drifted off in my lover's arms.

5-5. Final Fantasy

At about 10 a.m. the next morning, Ly and I emerged from the viewing room. I had just spent the hottest night ever with a woman. She was insatiable and could make me hard and ready over and over again. I felt like a young stud in her arms.

We had slept on and off in each other's arms during the night. I often woke up to find Ly caressing or fondling me back to life.

I was besotted with this incredible woman. She brought us both breakfast in bed and after we had enjoyed the fresh croissants and jam with a steaming café au lait, I took her for the fifth time that night.

As we left the room, it occurred to me that I hadn't turned on the screens once since I'd blanked them after Ly's arrival. If truth be told, I hadn't once thought about my wife during my night of passion with Ly. The thought that Anne was cheating on me with a woman still wrangled. The irony of the situation did strike me - how I had pushed her into having sex with several men, yet was feeling hurt and upset because she had taken a female lover without my knowledge. "It was different," I argued to myself, "she was doing it behind my back, without telling me."

I walked hand in hand with Ly through the corridors back to the front of the house. One of the servers from last night opened the front doors and indicated the car waiting for us.

"Is my wife coming?" I asked the server.

"Madame has already left, Sir." he responded and opened the car door.

I stepped into the back seat and slid across to make room for Ly.

"Good bye, Matt," she said, "thank you for a lovely night."

"But Ly, I thought you'd come with me and we could talk about 'us' and the future." I looked at her imploringly.

"That's very sweet Matt, but I have to go home and get on with my studies."

"Well, let me give you a lift somewhere," I was desperately clutching at straws. I couldn't leave her now.

"There's no need Matt. But thank you for offering." She leaned into the car and kissed me softly on the lips. "Bye, Matt".

She turned and walked back to the house with the server who shut the door as the car pulled away.

"Fuck, fuck, fuck," I said slamming my fist on the seat in front of me.

"Sir?" the driver looked back at me.

"Sorry," I said, "I'm feeling a little emotional. It's been a long week."

"Very well, Sir. Home, Sir?"

"I suppose so," I said, "Unless you happen to know where Ly lives…"

"I'm sorry, Sir, I don't."

And with that he was silent the rest of our short journey.

Tears were welling in my eyes as I stared blindly out of the window. "I have to find her, I have to. She's meant for me."

Suddenly I felt elation. I knew where she studied, I knew her first name. I knew she was from Vietnam. "There can't be that many Vietnamese studying medicine at the local University," it occurred to me.

"I will find her and make her mine," I said defiantly out loud as we pulled up to my door.

"Yes, Sir," the driver replied.

5-6. Future Shock - *Anne's Diary continues…*

I woke up a couple of hours after my earth-shattering orgasm to find Giuliana watching me sleep. We were still in the position I'd fallen asleep in.

"Hi, sleepy head," she said and kissed me lovingly.

My first words to her were "My God, Giuliana, you are an unbelievable lover. How did you do that?"

"Easy really," she said, "I'm in love and I want to give you everything I can."

I kissed her and pulled her close to me. I so wanted to reciprocate, but wasn't sure I could live up to her skills. But how hard could it be to make love to a woman. I know where all the bits are, it's just a bit strange finding them on your lover.

As we kissed I felt my passion surge again. To tell the truth, I could have an orgasm like that any time. I could still feel the aftershock, I was sure.

My hands began roaming over Giuliana's body. I caressed her soft fleshy breasts and pulled and tweaked her nipples in the way I liked. It seemed to work, because her tongue began to probe more deeply into my willing mouth.

I pulled away from her kiss and pulled the sheet off her to take in her body.

My fingers played with her nipples as I looked at her. They were so beautifully rigid. I had to take them in my mouth. I fell on them with my lips, tongue and teeth. As I lovingly teased each one in turn, Giuliana squirmed and moaned.

While my mouth concentrated on her divine breasts, my fingers moved down to the soft, warm, soft warm bushy spot between her legs. She was wet and open and my fingers slipped in with ease. I moved in and out gently, then brought my fingers up to my nose and sniffed the Giuliana's aroma, before slipping them into my mouth and sucking them dry.

Giuliana sat up and kissed me with passion, slipping her tongue in my mouth so she could taste herself.

I gave her nipples one last suck before moving my head down between her legs. I put a pillow under her buttocks and knelt between her legs. My fingers caressed her wet pussy lips and gently flicked her clitoris. I smiled at her and she looked at me lovingly.

Over the years I had often fantasized about kissing a woman's pussy. I had never acted on it, nor told anyone about it. I had also enjoyed checking out women that I found attractive, but I had never considered myself bi, let alone lesbian. As I stared down at Giuliana's pussy and looked into her eyes, I was feeling so passionate about her. There was even a feeling of love in my heart. I wanted to make this woman feel like she had made me feel earlier. I wanted to give her my passion.

Instead of diving in like a man, I kissed her gently on the thigh, little fairy kisses moving closer and closer to the prize. I did the same on the other leg. I kissed the hair around her pussy, licking the space between her thighs and her body and moving inward towards her lips, but stopping before I got there. As I moved down her pussy I pushed my tongue into the crack of her ass making her giggle and wriggle as I did. From there I ran my tongue slowly upwards over her outer lips up and over her clitoris. Very lightly, very slowly. I did this several times.

The aroma from her pussy was arousing me. She smelt sweet, yet musky. As I teased her pussy lips I could feel them opening slightly. The next time I moved slowly upwards, my tongue slipped slightly inside and liberated some of her juices. I tasted the dribbles on my tongue and knew I would be doing this often.

I decided to go back and tease her nipples again and to let Giuliana taste herself again on my lips and tongue. She kissed me greedily and moaned when I kissed and sucked on her nipples again. I kissed around her areolae and licked and sucked on her breasts, teasing her unapologetically.

It aroused me knowing that she also had sensitive nipples like mine. I found myself thinking that one day I would definitely make her come by only touching her breasts.

"So, I would be seeing Giuliana, again," I thought. I felt happy inside at such an idea.

Slowly, slowly I adored her breasts with my lips and tongue, before kissing and sucking my way south again.

I circled her labia several times and then pushed my tongue into her. She shrieked in delight and pulled my head closer to her pussy. I sucked her labia and bit and pulled on them before plunging my tongue back inside her. With each thrust she spasmed slightly.

As I moved up her pussy and licked her clitoris, she pulled my head again forcefully against her clit. I licked it and twirled it then sucked on it. Giuliana squealed and pulled my head closer. She seemed to love the sucking, so that's what I did. At one point I pushed a couple of fingers into her pussy and moved them in and out.

The combination of sucking on her clit, swirling my tongue over it and moving my fingers in and out had her squirming and squealing. Suddenly, she let out a massive scream and pulled my head hard towards her clit, before pushing me back and shuddering to a huge orgasm. I pressed my tongue hard on her clitoris and stopped moving my fingers. She continued to shudder for several seconds, before relaxing backwards onto the bed. As she fell back she pulled me up to her and kissed me passionately on the lips. I was covered in her juices, but she didn't seem to mind.

I lay on top of her and we both fell asleep in each other's arms wondering how I was going to introduce Giuliana to Matt.

"Oh, God, Matt," I thought, "He's probably wondering why I'm not letting him see the feed. He'll be imagining Christophe rogering me in every hole."

But somehow I felt soothed by Giuliana's soft breathing and a glow of love passed through me as I looked at the woman in my arms.

5-7. Burning Bridges

"Anne," I'm home, I shouted as I stepped through the door.

No answer.

"Fuck that," I said, "where the fuck is she?"

"Anne," I shouted more loudly, walking through the house. I stepped into our bedroom. There she was busy stuffing clothes into a suitcase.

"Hi Matt, I was hoping you'd get here soon" Anne said, as I walked in the bedroom.

"Why didn't you answer? I shouted twice."

"Sorry, I didn't hear you, I was a bit preoccupied and I'm in a hurry."

"What the fuck are you doing? Has this got something to do with that bitch you were kissing last night?"

"Kissing? You saw that?"

"Yes, I did. And I heard her tell you she loved you."

"You saw everything last night?"

"I saw enough before I turned it off."

"So you'd have been happy to watch me being mauled and

fucked by some stud, but you couldn't face me being kissed by a woman, is that it?"

"No that's not it, it's totally different. A meaningless fuck for pleasure and nothing else is so very different."

"Really? For the last few days I have played out your fantasy. I've taken it further than even you had imagined. I've done things I've would never have even contemplated a week ago. And now you're pissed off because I kissed a friend and want to spend a week with her."

"It looks like she's a fucking lot more than a friend. Do you love her?"

"Oh, Matt, what a question. Yes, I'm attracted to her and after all that happened this week I just wanted to get away."

"How long has this been going on?"

"What do you mean, 'going on', there's nothing going on. We met yesterday and now I'm going to her parents' house near Carrara for a week's holiday."

"The fuck you are."

"Matt, After all I've done for you this week I deserve this. I'll be back next week. I need the time to think about all that's happened.

"But, you can't just run off…"

"I'm not running off. Giuliana asked me to come with her. I thought it would be fun to see Italy. You start your project in a few days, so I'll hardly see you anyway."

"So fucking Giuliana, who you've known for 24 hours, is going to whisk you off on a romantic trip to Italy."

"Matt, are you jealous? Why weren't you jealous when Pascal fucked my cunt and ass red raw; when Antoine stuffed his thick prick in my cunt; when the crowd last night fondled me all over as I stood naked in front of them? I don't get it."

"Look Anne, I was jealous of Pascal and Antoine."

"You were? Why?

"I was jealous because I was worried I'd lose you. The fantasy of seeing you expose yourself and seeing you being fucked by another man is so erotic. Seeing it happen, or even hearing about it happen, makes me so hard. But at the back of my mind I couldn't get rid of the feeling that you'd prefer your new lover. And when you said Antoine had given you the best fuck ever, I was a mess."

"Why didn't you say something?" Anne said, putting her hand on my shoulder.

"There just wasn't time, everything happened so quickly, and you were so high on the sex and stuff. I felt you were having the time of your life."

Anne took me in her arms.

"But, the reason it felt like the best sex ever was purely because of the situation. It was part of your fantasy. I was living your dream and got totally carried away in the moment. Other than for your pleasure and mine it was meaningless."

"Deep down, I know that," I said, "but I can't help the fears. And then when I heard that this Italian woman loves you, I freaked."

"Matt, listen. Grant me this week. I need the time to recover. I also need the time to work out my feelings. Living out your fantasy was challenging, but I have to admit I enjoyed it. I uncovered a submissive side that I found rather erotic, and I discovered - because of you - that my body gives me power over men, and women too. I rather enjoy that side of things."

"So you're not leaving me?"

"No, I'm not. Do you think after fifteen years of marriage I'd just up and go on a whim, and what's more with a woman? Give me some credit, at least."

The doorbell rang.

That'll be Giuliana. Anne clicked her case shut. She turned to me and kissed me full on the lips. I put my arms around her and could feel the tears welling up.

"I'll be back in a week," she said, "and I'll call you every day."

I watched as she wheeled her suitcase click-clacking on her heels through the house to the front door. She looked so sexy. She was wearing a flared skirt and simple v-neck t-shirt and of course she had her favorite heels on.

I stood at the end of the corridor. I wasn't keen on meeting this Giuliana. I might say something I'd regret.

Anne opened the door.

"Hello," said Ly, "you must be Matt's wife," and held out her hand.

Anne didn't take it and looked over her shoulder at me.

"And you are?" Anne bristled visibly.

I ran quickly to Anne's side.

"Hello Ly, this is Ly," I said to Anne, "we met last night at The Club."

"Oh did you, is she one of the perks?"

Anne pushed past Ly with her case.

"I'll call you, have a lovely week. You too, Ly."

Ly and I watched her walk down the hill. A car pulled up beside her after a couple of minutes and the Italian woman from last night jumped out and helped Anne put her suitcase in the back. The woman kissed my wife on the lips and embraced her. Laughing together they got into the car and it raced off up the hill. Anne was talking avidly with the Italian when the car passed us. She didn't look our way.

Ly turned to me when the car had gone past.

"Sorry, Matt, I hope I didn't cause any problems."

"Not at all, come in," I said, "I'm really so very happy to see you."

I shut the door and looked at her. Her delicious puffy nipples were highlighted by the tank top she was wearing and her shapely legs looked stunning against her short pastel skirt.

Ly put her arms round my neck and kissed me. Her tongue on my lips made me instantly hard. I eagerly wrapped my arms around her and kissed her back.

"Matt," she said, "I've been thinking about what you said, I think we should sit and talk about us and about our future".

Suddenly the next week looked so much better.

.

www.ingramcontent.com/pod-product-compliance
Lightning Source LLC
Chambersburg PA
CBHW021011180626
46814CB00003B/1248